Praise for *Anything But Groovy*

Anything but Groovy takes us all back to better times. And for me that was worth the read alone. Every page resonated with me. Amanda Lauer has done an amazing job of creating a time that many lived through. So wonderfully done that you felt as if you were there. I can't say enough about this story. So wonderful. So unique. By the end, I didn't want to come back to 2020. My highest praise!
Cary Solomon, writer/director/producer of *Unplanned* (The Abby Johnson story), *God's Not Dead* and other award-winning films

Anything But Groovy is a coming of age novel with touches of history and an intriguing Freaky Friday type of storyline. Lauer expertly captures the details of the 70s in a story that modern teens will thoroughly enjoy as well. This glimpse into a parent's childhood was such a clever way to explore the walking-a-mile-in-another's-shoes theme. This novel would make a fabulous book for mothers and daughters to enjoy together because it is simply groovy.

Leslea Wahl, author of the award-winning teen novel The Perfect Blindside.

Morgan, our main character, finds herself in a not-so-ordinary fish-out-of-water situation and has to fight her way through seventh grade in the '70s. Though lighthearted and humorous most of the times, this story also focuses on real problems like bullying. A must read for teenagers; friendship, family life and the dazzling 70s, what else could you wish for?
Sophie Habsburg-Lothringen

If you were a *Brady Bunch* fan, you ought to give *Anything But Groovy* to your kids. An accidental bounce through time has the '70s groove being witnessed by a '20s kid. A fun time-warp story that reveals what we old folks lived through in our youth."

Michelle Buckman, award-winning author

Judy,
Enjoy this
groovy trip
back in time!

Anything But Groovy

A Novel

By Amanda Lauer

Full Quiver Publishing
Pakenham ON

This book is a work of fiction. Although the setting for this novel takes place in the 1970s, some of the names, characters and incidents are products of the author's imagination. Real events and characters are used fictitiously.

Anything But Groovy
copyright 2021
by Amanda Lauer

Published by Full Quiver Publishing
PO Box 244
Pakenham, Ontario K0A 2X0

ISBN Number: 978-1-987970-22-7
Printed and bound in the USA

Front Cover photo courtesy Amanda Lauer
Back cover photo negatives courtesy Amanda Lauer
Cover design: James Hrkach/Amanda Lauer

NATIONAL LIBRARY OF CANADA
CATALOGUING IN PUBLICATION

Published by FQ Publishing
A Division of Innate Productions

For my friends, classmates, lay teachers, religious sisters, staff and priests from St. John Elementary School. The experiences we shared helped make me the person that I am today.

Chapter 1

With my focus on the direction of the spike, I didn't notice Hailey land off-balance. The next thing I knew, she slammed into me, and my head bounced off the gleaming hardwood floor.

Just what I need, a huge goose egg for the first day of school tomorrow. It took a few seconds to shake away the stars floating in front of my eyes.

Grabbing Hailey's extended hand, I accepted her apology and popped up into position for the next serve. A whistle shrilled. Coach called it a night.

That wasn't good. Tryouts for club volleyball were only a week away. Competition for the libero spot was intense. The last thing I needed was to look like a wuss. If they thought I was injured, the coaches would hand the spot to Sydney in a heartbeat.

It's not that Sydney didn't deserve a place on the team, but I'd been busting my tail in the weight room and at open gyms all summer trying to earn my way onto the elite squad.

Besides, after the craptastic last two weeks, I deserved to have something go right in my life. One stupid picture and I was the laughingstock of social media.

The afternoon at the pool the week before last had started off well enough. Then came the swimsuit malfunction. The bell had sounded for everyone to clear the pool for the ten-minute mandatory lifeguard break. As I pushed myself up onto the concrete ledge, the tie came loose on my bikini bottom, and I ended up mooning the entire city. Madison, the quintessential "mean girl" in our class, happened to have her phone at hand and got a shot before I could pull the back end of my suit up.

That picture made the cyberspace rounds before I even got back to the house. Now I'm dubbed "The Coppertone Girl," after some dumb suntan lotion ad from when Mom was a kid. Even people I don't know are calling me Copper. If I was a redhead, it might be cute, but seeing that I'm not, it was just plain embarrassing.

And, if that wasn't bad enough, Trinity had zero empathy for me. All those times I came to her rescue when she was having boy drama in sixth grade, and this was how I get repaid? *Some best friend she is.*

With her height, Trinity was an awesome right-sider hitter. *What if she made the team and I didn't?* Waiting for Mom to pull up to the curb, a sigh escaped my lips.

Volleyball was a bust, who knew what would happen with me and Trinity, summer was over, and I was scheduled to take the PSATs next week. Even though I'm only going into seventh grade, Dad says that "bright students" need to start the process in middle school to get a leg up applying for college. *Seriously, I'd like to see one actual thirteen-year-old thinking about college applications.*

On top of that, we had school pictures in the morning. I'd look like an alien if I had some huge bump coming out of the side of my head. *All this stress and school hasn't even started yet.*

"How was practice?" Mom inquired when I slid onto

the passenger seat of the SUV.

"It was all right until I got wiped out by Hailey."

"Oh my gosh. Are you okay, Morgan?"

"I'm fine. It was no big deal."

Buckled in, I posted a picture of me sitting on the volleyball court, giving the thumbs up. "*Gym floor = 1, Morgan Miller = 0.*" Maybe if I put this out there and poked some fun at myself, the popularity of the Coppertone picture would diminish.

"Didn't you just get done talking with your friends?"

"Yah," I replied, eyes locked on the screen.

"What are you texting about now?"

Instinctively, my eyes rolled. "Wasn't texting… posting a picture."

Mom gave that, "Really, Morgan?" sigh before pulling out onto the street.

Is it just her, or is every teenager's mom weirdly interested in their kids' lives?

My focus riveted back to the phone. A few blocks into the trip home, Mom spoke up again. "Other than getting wiped out, how was practice?"

"Lame."

"You know, Dad and I have put a lot of money into your 'lame' training the last two years."

Here we go again, the my-parents-never-even-went-to-one-of-my-sporting-events-in-my-life-let-alone-paid-for-professional-training speech.

Cutting her off before she could begin, I spouted out, "It's ridiculous, though, Mom. Why such an intense practice the night before the first day of school? Us girls didn't even get a minute to talk."

Mom gave me a doubtful look before turning her eyes to the road again. I went back to posting as we drove the last couple blocks.

At home, I tossed a bag of popcorn in the microwave, devoured half of it, scrolled through more pictures, sent a few texts for the final word of what everyone would be wearing to school in the morning, then took out my contacts. That done, I stepped into the downstairs bathroom to take a shower.

Afterwards, as I walked through the den, Mom patted a spot on the couch next to her. Instinctively, I took a seat.

"Remember when you were in grade school, and every day after school, you came home and sat on my lap and gave me a report with every last detail of your day?"

"Uh-huh," I replied.

"I miss those days," Mom noted.

I dropped my head to her shoulder.

"Are you looking forward to your first day of seventh grade?"

"I guess."

"It seems like it was just yesterday when I was starting junior high."

"They don't call it junior high anymore, Mom. It's middle school."

"I know; old habits die hard."

I sank further into the couch, snuggling into Mom's side.

"Are you worried about school?" she inquired.

"Not necessarily. There's just so much going on right now. Things are more complicated than when you were growing up. There's a lot more pressure on kids nowadays."

"Trust me. We had our share of pressure then too. It's just different than it is today."

I looked at her skeptically.

"Seventh grade was one of my most challenging years," she added.

"What happened?"

"Just like for you, it wasn't just one thing. There was school, Girl Scouts, friend issues, family issues, and...classmate issues."

"Classmate issues?"

Mom pulled me into her arms. "That's a story for another time. But, let me say this, in the words of Winnie the Pooh's friend, Christopher Robin, 'You are braver than you believe, stronger than you seem, and smarter than you think.'"

She gave me a reassuring hug. "I wish someone would have told me that when I was your age," she whispered in my ear.

I pulled back to look at her. The expression in her eyes was hard to decipher. *Regret? Sadness*?

"Good night, Morgan."

"Thanks, Mom," I said, hugging her tightly. "Night, love you!"

"Love you, too."

Chapter 2

Head throbbing, I placed my phone face down on the nightstand and turned off the lamp. I must have fallen asleep immediately because I never even heard Mom and Dad come upstairs to tuck Brock and Brayden into bed.

The first thing that came to mind when I woke up in the morning was the collision the night before. Eyes still closed; I tentatively patted my skull front to back. The only thing out of place was my hair, which felt kind of weird. No goose egg, though, thank goodness. As long as I could pull off a genuine smile, school pictures should be all right.

One last stretch and my eyes popped open. Peering at the plastered ceiling overhead, I considered the upcoming day. It was cool starting seventh grade and finally being in middle school. Even if we were in the same building that we'd been in since Pre-K, we were now upperclassmen. *Sweet!*

Hopefully, I'd have a better experience than it sounded like Mom had. There were some good things going for it already. I still felt like I had a decent chance to make the volleyball team. At school, every seventh-grader was going to be issued a new tablet, and, what us girls were most looking forward to, we would now be allowed to slow dance with boys at the socials.

Taking a deep breath in anticipation, I waited for

my phone to play my go-to wake-up song. Nothing. Must have been earlier than I thought. After a good stretch, I rolled over.

My hand patted the top of the nightstand. The phone was gone. *Are you kidding me?* Here I thought Mom and me had such a great bonding experience last night, and now she goes and swipes my phone? She probably took it downstairs and put it on the kitchen countertop. It was part of her "tough love" social media policy that she'd heard about on some Christian radio station. Since she and Dad were paying for the device, they felt like they could monitor my phone usage. In other words, spy on me.

How was I supposed to be a "responsible young lady" and get myself up for school if I didn't have my phone alarm? I glanced back at my nightstand. My eyes opened wider. Even without my glasses, I spotted something that hadn't been there when I went to bed.

An alarm clock. An old-fashioned one like Grandma had with a round face, black numbers, four gold feet, two bells on top and a loud ticker. Was this Mom's idea of a joke?

A second later, it went off. *Holy crap*, it was loud enough to wake the dead. I rolled over and grabbed it. The clock vibrated in my hand as I tried to figure out how to turn the stupid thing off. Jamming the little peg into its back, the noise finally stopped.

Heart racing, I set the offending thing down and reached for my glasses. Picking them up, it didn't take more than a second to realize that they weren't mine. These weren't the designer frames that I'd just gotten from the one-hour glasses place. This pair was brown plastic with six-sided lenses. Something like the hipsters were wearing. Like adult hipsters, not middle schoolers. Out of curiosity, I put them on. Surprisingly, they seemed to be close to my own prescription.

Was this supposed to be a back-to-school joke? Mom was probably downstairs laughing her rear-end off right now. I swung my legs out of bed. Glancing around the room with crystal-clear vision, the breath caught in my throat.

There was definitely something weird going on. Instead of taupe-colored walls, my Pottery Barn comforter, cream-colored window blinds and hardwood floors, I saw yellow walls, a white pull-down window shade, frilly eyelet curtains, an orange chenille bedspread and lime-green wall-to-wall shag carpeting. It looked like a scene from *The Spy Who Shagged Me.*

I scooted off the bed and slowly turned in a circle to take in the whole room. A poster hung above my bed. The picture showed some teenage guy. With the nerdy glasses, I read the signature at the top. "I love you, David." Who the heck was David? Peering closer, his face looked familiar. Was this the actor from *The Partridge Family* show that was on the classic TV network?

Someone was obviously trying to freak me out. Stepping over to the closet, I warily cracked open the door to see if that space was as messed up as the rest of my room.

Nothing jumped out at me, but when I opened the door all the way, I could see my reflection in the full-length mirror. My jaw dropped, and my eyes bugged out.

This was not what I was wearing when I went to bed last night. Instead of my yoga pants and volleyball camp t-shirt, I was dressed in a nightgown. I tilted my chin up to see my whole reflection. *My hair, what the heck?* I stepped closer to the mirror and pulled the cord dangling overhead to turn on the light fixture.

"Oh... my... gosh." I must have hit my head a lot harder than I thought.

Chapter 3

A knock on my bedroom door almost made me jump out of my skin. Backing out of the closet, I crept toward the door, pausing a second and taking a deep breath so I didn't look like I was flipping out.

Self-consciously smoothing my hair down, I cracked the door open.

Grandma? "What are you doing here?" I blurted out.

"Are you surprised I'm up so early?" she asked cheerily.

"Um, I guess, but, like, why are you here at all?"

"Since it's the first day of school, I wanted to make sure you were up and getting ready."

That made no sense. She didn't care any other time of the year if I was up or not. Why would she come over today to check?

But that wasn't the biggest issue. There was something weird about her. Her voice was the same, but she looked way different.

"Did you dye your hair?"

Grandma put her hand to her head. "Does it look too dark? I put a fall on this morning. It's mahogany. I thought it'd be the closest match to my real hair color."

"A fall? You mean like hair extensions?"

"I guess you could call it that. A few of the girls

from the base got them, so I thought I'd get one too. You like it?"

The base? Was she losing it? The radar base that Grandpa had worked at had been closed since before I was born.

Mechanically, I nodded.

When we'd picked Grandma up for church Sunday, her hair had been its normal mix of gray and white. I looked closer at her eyebrows. Holy cow! They were dyed to match her hair. The skin on her face was so smooth. She must've had a facial too.

What had possessed her to make the drastic change? Was she seeing someone? She'd never remarried after Grandpa left her. Maybe she'd met some guy at the assisted living facility.

At the moment, though, I had bigger things to worry about, so I told Grandma that I'd see her downstairs in a bit. I quickly made the bed and went to open the white plastic shade. After a good tug, it sprung up and hit the top of the window frame. If Brock and Brayden hadn't been awake before, they would be now.

Sunshine illuminated the dresser top. A couple figurines, including a bear-shaped bottle of perfume, sat on an oval mirrored tray. Where was my stuff?

A tiny doll, less than an inch tall, was encased in a locket attached to a gold necklace. Her head was almost as big as the rest of her body. She had big yellow eyes outlined in black, pink cheeks, blond pigtails that went to her feet, a peach-colored dress trimmed in gold glitter, and she smelled like flowers.

Obviously, Mom and Dad were playing a prank on

me. But why today, of all days? Regardless, I had to get ready for school. Opening the top dresser drawer, my jaw dropped in dismay. One after another, I tugged the other drawers open. All my clothes were gone. Other pieces took their place. There were jeans and corduroys with wide leg openings, another nightgown, colored knee-high socks, white tube socks with stripes around the tops, and a bunch of t-shirts, including a vintage Adidas one.

This looked like stuff that Mom wore when she was a kid. Where'd they ever find it? And how did I not hear them when they made the swap last night? That knock to the head must've really conked me out.

The next find was classic. Waist-high days-of-the-week undies. I had no idea they made them my size. Short-sleeved crew neck undershirts rounded out the selection.

As weirded out as I was, curiosity got the better of me, and I stepped back to the closet to see what it held. On the far left was a quilted bathrobe. Next to that were several long-sleeve, button-down shirts, including some flannel ones. On the right side hung short-sleeve shirts. A few were button-down and a couple were pullover styles.

Since I needed to put something on until I found my real clothes, I grabbed a shirt off a metal hanger with the price tag still attached, a pair of hippy jeans, knee-highs, the Monday undies and an undershirt. No sports bras? *Really, Mom? You could have at least left one.*

Surprisingly enough, everything fit. I took one last look at the outfit in the mirror. *Rocking the '70s look, if I have to say so myself.* Maybe I'd keep the ensemble for spirit week next January when we'd get to dress up in clothes from different generations.

That sense of satisfaction lasted for all of two seconds until the reflection of my hair came into view. Looking at the chop job, with three distinct layers — bangs, a ledge just under my ears, and longer hair in the back that touched my collar — I screeched in frustration. *There is no way on earth I'm getting my pictures taken today.* I'll skip out and wait for retake day.

This had to be Mom's doing. What would possibly possess her to pull such a stunt? *I just shared with her last night how much pressure I'm under.* With school starting, there'll be a boatload of homework every night, another week preparing for volleyball tryouts, the never-ending friend and classmate drama, and the job of restoring my damaged social media image. She had no idea what it was like being a teenager now compared to her *Happy Days* life.

When I see her downstairs, there'll be no holding back. I'll put even the most hideous bridezilla to shame.

Seeing a stack of hair things on the closet shelf, I grabbed a plastic, brown headband and shoved it onto my head to push the middle layer of hair back to blend in with the back layer. Pictures or no, there was no way I'd be caught in public with this disastrous chop job.

Hearing the boys stirring, I flung open my bedroom door. The sight in front of me caused me to freeze mid-step. It was two boys all right, just not Brock and Brayden. These guys were high-school age.

They rammed each other in an attempt to get into the bathroom first.

"Out of the way, spaz," said the taller boy.

"I need the bathroom first, jerk face. Have to shave," said the other boy, who seemed to be the younger of the two.

"Robbie and Howie, stop that arguing now," came Grandma's voice from downstairs.

Robbie and Howie? Those were the nicknames that Grandma had for Uncle Robert and Uncle Howard. She really was losing her marbles.

"Yes, Mom," they said in unison while still pushing each other.

Mom?

With one last shove, the older boy went back toward the bedroom on the front side of the house. "Since you only have two hairs, it'll take five seconds to shave them off, babyface. Better be out in two minutes, or I'm coming in after you."

"You and what army, Howie?"

The only answer the younger guy got was the sound of a bedroom door slamming.

I stared at the kid in the hallway. What was he doing in our house?

"Take a picture; it'll last longer," he spat out before stepping into the bathroom and shutting the door firmly behind him.

My mind spun. This guy looked like a teenage, shaggy-haired version of Uncle Robert. The other guy resembled Uncle Howard. But the Howard I knew had gray-streaked hair, wore trendy glasses, and was out of shape after spending his career sitting at a desk. And that guy never raised his voice, even when his son was going bonkers.

While I processed the scene I'd just witnessed, I heard slippered footsteps coming up the stairs. Grandma stepped into the hallway and noticed me standing by my bedroom door.

"You're going to have to jog to school if you don't get moving."

Jog? Wasn't I getting a ride?

My feet were rooted to the hallway floor.

"I'm not joking, young lady. You have to leave in ten minutes, or you'll be late."

My eyes widened in disbelief.

"Get truckin'."

The woman had seriously lost it. What the heck did get truckin' mean, and why was she bossing me around?

"Mo-o-o-m!"

Chapter 4

Grandma crossed her arms in front of her and nodded toward the staircase. Obediently, I went down the stairs, not wanting to send her off the deep end by pointing out that she was crazy. That'd be Mom's job.

Mom and Dad were probably waiting in the kitchen for me to show up in my groovy outfit. They'd been known to pull a prank or two on us kids, but they outdid themselves today. Wonder where they found the Uncle Howard and Uncle Robert clones?

Brock and Brayden were nowhere in sight. They were probably holed up in their bedrooms, waiting to sneak downstairs to see me go off on Mom and Dad. Which was exactly what I was gearing up to do. Seriously, of all days, why would they pull this crap on the first day of school?

Tiffany and Emory weren't going to believe it when I told them about my morning. We all knew our parents were uncool, but this stunt would give Mom and Dad the prize for being the most whack parents on the planet.

On the way down the steps, I glanced at the bookshelves lining the wall of the landing. Instead of Blu-rays and video games, the shelves were littered with trophies. I recognized Grandma's golf, volleyball, softball and bowling trophies that she normally displayed in her apartment. Grandpa's golf and bowling trophies were there too.

Was this a permanent exhibition or just part of the September Fool's Day joke? At the bottom of the steps, the piano was positioned in front of the side door where it'd been since Mom grew up in this house. At least something was the same.

After running my hands over the keys, I opened the glass door leading to the living room and dining room. Most mornings, Mom would be sitting by the table, checking her email when I came down. Her chair was empty today.

Dad usually left for work by seven-thirty. But, on the first day of school, he always went in late so he could take a picture of each of us kids standing on the back stoop before we piled into the SUV for the ride to school. The shot was mandatory for Mom's back-to-school scrapbook page.

After what they'd put me through today, I had no intention of smiling for any pictures, no matter what Dad did to make me laugh. It'd serve them right for trying to mess up my first day of seventh grade.

The kitchen was deserted too. An empty mug sat on the kitchen table, so Dad had been there. Hearing a car running, I stepped out the back door onto the concrete stoop.

Some guy was pulling the garage door shut using the handle. The opener must be broken. Then confusion really set in. Why was some dude, in a strange vehicle, shutting our garage door?

The car looked like one that Grandma admired at the old car shows. I recognized the logo. Vintage Chevy, Grandma's favorite. Could it be hers? Maybe that's why she stopped by today, to show off her new wheels.

I got a full view of the guy when he stepped away from the garage. Orange-flared pants and a matching orange-flowered shirt unbuttoned halfway down his hairy chest. Black hair tucked behind his ears and Elvis sideburns. *Is this guy for real?*

Slipping behind the wheel, he backed the car out of the gravel driveway and onto the street. Before pulling away, he gave me a wave. My eyes widened further. Holy crap, the guy looked like the young Grandpa in the black and white pictures from Mom's scrapbooks.

Mechanically, I returned the wave. Once he took off, I went back into the house, noticing for the first time that our wooden kitchen table and chairs had been replaced with metal furniture. The table surface had gold geometric designs and metal edging. Six metal chairs had plastic seats with the same design as the tabletop.

Looking on either side of the galley kitchen, our appliances had been swapped out with olive green ones. Something weird was going on. Either I was being punked, or aliens had taken over our house.

"Mom?" I said in a low voice. There was no answer. "Dad?" Still, no answer. *Where is everybody?*

In a full-blown panic, I belted out at the top of my lungs, "Da-a-a-ddy!"

Chapter 5

I heard one set of footsteps rushing up from the basement and two sets of footsteps thundering down from upstairs. Grandma came flying through the den and front entryway and came to a halt in front of me.

"What on earth is going on?" she gasped.

She was the last person that I wanted to see. "Where's Dad?"

"He just left for work. You saw him pull out of the driveway."

"No, I didn't," I replied, trying to hold back the tears.

"You waved goodbye. I noticed when I was bringing the wash out."

"That wasn't Dad," I replied emphatically.

Grandma looked at me, her brow furrowed. Stepping closer, she brought her hand to my forehead. "Are you feeling okay?"

I flinched when she touched me. "I feel fine," I said, pulling away.

Two voices came from behind me.

"What gives?"

"Who's screaming like a banshee down here?"

I knew those voices. It was the two guys from upstairs. I plastered myself against the back door. Panic set in. My eyes bugged out, and tears formed on my lower eyelids.

The boys gawked at me like I was nuts. I looked at them like they were zombies. Grandma glanced between the three of us in confusion.

"All right, you two," she said, staring directly at the guys. "What gives?

"Why ask us? She's the one spazzing out," replied the older guy.

"She was perfectly normal at supper yesterday, and now she's not," said Grandma. "You played Kick-the-Can last night. Were you playing too rough? Did she get hurt?"

"Right, Ma," said the younger guy sarcastically. "If one of us had laid a hand on her, she'd been in here tattling as soon as the streetlights came on."

"We didn't do anything to her," added the other kid. "She's just a big cry baby."

"Am not!" I replied emphatically. *Who the heck are these guys, and why are they being so mean?*

My head began to pound. Coach was worried that I'd gotten a concussion at volleyball practice. Maybe I actually did. I felt really out of it.

"You two, go upstairs and finish getting ready for school," said Grandma, pointing the guys toward the dining room. "As for you, young lady, I'm keeping an eye on you. Why don't you have some breakfast? That may make you feel better."

I nodded, sniffed back my tears, and walked to the kitchen cabinet. Peering inside, I found Pink Panther Flakes, Punch Crunch and Sugar Frosted Flakes. *Interesting selection.* White bowls with a Colonial pattern had replaced the usual Fiestaware in the cupboard. I opened the fridge to grab the milk. *Whole milk?*

The Sugar Frosted Flakes were the closest thing to normal cereal, so I poured a bowl and sat down to eat. It tasted like real food, so this wasn't a dream. With Grandma watching, I dutifully ate the whole bowl. When I finished, I brought it over to the dishwasher.

Or, where the dishwasher was supposed to be.

"Where's the dishwasher?"

"You're looking at her," said Grandma. She cocked her head and perused me head to toe. "Are you sure you feel fine?"

I nodded slightly.

Grandma stepped into the walk-in closet by the back door and came out with a thick, clear plastic bag. Inside were three spiral-bound notebooks, two new pencils, three black Bic pens, a wooden ruler, a bottle of Elmer's glue, and a huge box of crayons.

"Everything's packed. I'll leave this on the table for you. Get your teeth brushed and get a move on."

Without knowing what else to do, I did as she commanded. My electric toothbrush was missing, so I grabbed a pink manual toothbrush from a silver cup holder screwed to the bathroom wall. Looking through the medicine cabinet, I found toothpaste, plus V-05 hair stuff, cloth Band-Aids, a glass bottle of aspirin, and a brown glass bottle of hydrogen peroxide. My contacts were missing.

I could deal with the lame hairdo, but the nerdy glassed were not acceptable.

"Where are my contacts?" I yelled down the stairs.

"We didn't order them. You said the glass hurt your eyes."

Glass? Aren't contacts plastic? I had no recollection of that conversation. Par for the course today. Whatever. I just needed to go through the motions until I figured out what was going on.

Striding back through the kitchen, Grandma handed me the bag.

"Out you go!"

I stopped and looked at her expectantly.

"What?" she asked.

"Do you have the keys?"

"What keys?"

"To the car."

She looked at me askance. "No. Dad has them."

"How am I going to get to school?" I asked, scrunching up my eyebrows.

"The same way you always do. Walk."

"You're not driving me?"

Grandma held the back of her hand up to my forehead and then to each of my cheeks. "If it wasn't the first day of school, I'd bring you to the clinic. You still seem a bit off."

That was an understatement if I'd ever heard one.

Opening the screen door, Grandma shooed me out the back. I went down the concrete steps and started down the driveway. Halfway to the sidewalk, I heard her call out.

"Have a great day, Ally! See you after school!"

I stopped dead in my tracks. Grandma thought that I was Mom. Things were way worse than I imagined.

Chapter 6

Not knowing what else to do, I set off in the direction of St. Joseph Elementary School. It was only a few blocks from our house, but Mom had always driven me and the boys.

Speaking of those two, I still hadn't seen Brock or Brayden.

This day was seriously messed up. Giving a sigh, I meandered past our next-door neighbor's house. It'd been quiet there since Mr. Olson passed away. It was weird not seeing him sitting on his back step, having a smoke and hacking his lungs out.

There were several junker cars in their driveway. Maybe the kids were visiting Mrs. Olson. With the windows open, I could hear talking and yelling. Wendy was probably in town with her little ones. Three kids, three dads, no husband. She was one busy lady.

The next house was Mr. Henderson's, the sheriff's deputy. A Lassie-type dog lounged on the sidewalk. *When'd he get a dog?* Shrugging my shoulders, I paused, scratched the dog behind its ears and then kept going.

Two blocks down, I turned left at the public grade school, South Elementary. The playground swarmed with kids. I swore half of them had ADD. Mom said Uncle Robert was hyperactive as a kid too. He did impulsive things like walk across active railroad bridges, hitchhike or shoplift for the thrill of it.

As an adult, he was really messed up. He'd gotten into pot in college, was married and divorced twice, had an addiction to gambling and booze, and was living on the streets somewhere. It was sad how his life turned out.

Thinking of Mom, where was she? Would she have taken Brock and Brayden to school without me? Hopefully, she was there already with a change of clothes and a pair of contacts for me. She's been so annoying lately. But this takes the cake.

St. Joseph's came into view. Something wasn't right. Where was the fieldhouse? We were just there last night at volleyball practice. All I saw in front of me was a patch of blacktop and some old-school playground equipment. Merry-go-round, climbing tower, two sets of swings and a metal slide.

Yelling and laughing kids were sprawled all over the playground. We had only ten kids in each grade at St. Joseph's. Where'd all the rest of these kids come from?

Maybe the new glasses were making my vision wacky. *I need to find Mom.* Crossing the street, I walked to the front of the school. Finally, something I recognized. Same brick building, same double glass doors, same tile in the entryway.

The first floor was packed with more kids. Parents were few and far between. A sister in an old-fashioned habit stood outside the first-grade classroom, checking names off a list when students entered the room. Brayden was going to have a sister for a teacher? The kind with a veil and everything? Crazy.

As far as I could see, he wasn't in the room, so I kept going down the hall. Maybe Mom was dropping Brock off first. I passed by the second-grade classroom and saw my old teacher, Mrs. Clark. She glanced up from hugging one of her students, saw me and waved.

My jaw nearly hit the ground. The rest and relaxation over the summer must've done her a world of good. She looked even younger than when I had her as a teacher.

Bounding up a half-dozen steps, I stood in the hallway of the second level, where the third- and fourth-grade classrooms were. Must have been some retirements over the summer; I didn't recognize any of the teachers. I peeked inside Brock's room but didn't see him or his friends.

Where was everyone today? Most likely, Mom's upstairs by my homeroom. Probably waiting with the boys to surprise me.

I went up the next flight of steps. The third level was just as packed as the first two, but I still didn't recognize anyone. It was like my world had been turned upside-down overnight.

Was this just some crazy dream? I pinched my arm. *Ouch!* So much for that theory. Okay, not dreaming. Dead? Probably not. Otherwise, Mrs. Clark wouldn't have acknowledged me.

Maybe it was that volleyball thing. *Do head injuries make people hallucinate?*

Trying my best not to freak out, I made my way through the crowd of kids and approached each door to examine the class lists. Some of the last names were familiar, but the first names didn't match up with anyone I knew.

There were lists for the fifth-graders, sixth-graders and eighth-graders, but I didn't see any for my grade. The only door left was one leading to the old auditorium on the top floor of the building.

A piece of paper was taped to the doorframe. Seventh Grade was handwritten at the top in block letters. Under the heading was a list of students' names. There were a lot more names than there should've been. Who were these kids?

Ackerman, Stacey; Caruso, Monica; Cavanaugh, Matt; Connors, Allison; Coopman, Lawrence; Dobransky, Jane; Donovan, Steven; Fischer, Kurt; Frederickson, Patty; Gale, Brenda; Gilbert, Rhonda; Hauser, Chris; Holtz, Vicky; Howell, Bobbi Jo; Keep, Kevin; Kohler, Greg; Kovac, Gina; Ledoux, Connie; Masterson, Eric; McFadden, McKenzie; McVee, Jeff; Meyer, Ronald; Mueller, Laura; Rogan, Theresa; Ruzek, Jonathon; Sanders, Sharon; Schaefer, Gary; Scherer, David; Schmidt, Richard; Schultz, Edward; Shoreman, Brian; Sperling, Rebecca; Stark, Sheila; Wickert, Andrew.

I took off my glasses. Squinting, I read the list again. *Connors, Allison? As in Ally?* That was Mom's maiden name. *This is not good.*

Chapter 7

Mouth gaping, I read the list a third time, looking at each individual name. Some of them seemed familiar. Vicky Holtz and Gina Kovac? Those were the names of Mom's two best friends when she was growing up.

This was either the most elaborate prank of all time, or I was going bananas. In a daze, I ascended the steps to the auditorium, cautiously peeking inside the door.

The stage, with its heavy crimson curtain, looked like it always had. But, instead of computer desks and chairs, there were a bunch of metal desks with wooden seats attached to them, filling the space.

Bookbag held tightly to my chest, I stepped into the room. A couple of kids smiled and said hi. There were bunches of students scattered throughout the space, including a group of six girls chatting in the far corner. One of them had the same shirt on like Mom's that I wore.

The girl leading their discussion glanced over at me. Indicating me with her head, the whole group glanced my way and burst into laughter.

My cheeks blazed. *What a bunch of bi-o...*

The bell rang, cutting that thought off. There was a mad scramble for desks. Following everyone else's lead, I secured a chair in the back-right corner of the room.

Kids swung open the tops of their desks and unloaded their bookbags. Following suit, I emptied mine as well. Out of the corner of my eye, I saw someone hustling into the room.

"Flying in late as per usual, Vicky?" inquired the teacher, another sister, who stood planted in front of the room. "Apparently, you don't live by the axiom, 'To be early is to be on time, to be on time is to be late, and to be late is to be forgotten.'"

"Actually, I live by the axiom, 'Better late than never,' Sister," she replied.

The other kids broke out in laughter.

"Fair enough," said the sister.

The girl dropped into the empty seat next to mine. I glanced her way and did a doubletake. She was the spitting image of Mom's friend, Mrs. Peterson. Vicky Peterson. If this is the Vicky Holtz whose name was on the class list, things were really topsy turvy.

Getting back on track, the sister continued. "As you can see, we've combined all the seventh-graders into one class this year." She glanced at the students. "For the first week of school, you'll keep a nameplate on your desk so the teachers that you haven't had before can learn your names."

She picked up the stack of nameplates from the podium and handed them to the kid sitting in the seat closest to her.

"Brian, grab your nameplate and then pass the rest along."

"Yes, Sister Cecilia."

Brian, Sister Cecilia. I committed the names to

memory in case there'd be a test.

"While you're doing that, I'd like to introduce you to our newest classmate." My heart constricted. *Is she going to single me out?* I clamped my lips together and stared straight ahead.

"Please welcome Tammy Obermeier." Sister Cecilia swept her hand in my direction.

Tammy Obermeier? I could feel eyes turning in my direction.

Make that, somewhat in my direction. Everyone was checking out the girl in the desk to my left. I turned and scoped her out, as well. Sister continued the introduction, but my mind wandered somewhere else.

It seemed like these kids knew me, but, other than the Mrs. Peterson mini-me, I didn't recognize any of them. *Where are my real classmates?*

As the kids welcomed Tammy, the nameplates circulated throughout the room. By the time the stack got to me, there were just six left. I thumbed through them without seeing my name. Down to the last one, I froze.

"Hey," said Vicky.

I couldn't get myself to respond.

"Hey," she said a little louder. "Take yours and hand the rest over."

I heard what she said but couldn't say anything.

"Four eyes," said some guy with a deep voice two desks over. "Can't you see out of those dorky glasses?"

His remark brought me out of my trance.

"Richard, there's no need for that," said Sister Cecilia.

I looked from the Richard guy to Sister Cecilia and then back down to the nameplate in my hand. Without glancing toward Vicky, I flung my arm toward her so she could grab the rest.

The buzzing I'd had in my ears earlier intensified. I blinked twice, but the words didn't change. ALLISON CONNORS.

Chapter 8

Transfixed, I stared at Mom's name on the nameplate. My mind swam as I tried wrapping my head around the situation.

Can you dream in 3D with all your senses intact?

A chill ran through me. *Could I be dead?* I rubbed my hands on my upper arms. Pretty sure dead people don't interact with live people. They probably don't get goosebumps.

Was I hallucinating because of the head injury last night? I ran my fingers through my hair. *No bump, couldn't have been that bad.*

I'd seen the movie *A Wrinkle in Time*. Was it possible that I was traveling through time? But time travelers stay in their own bodies. They don't hijack other people's bodies. Or do they?

"Allison." The whispered comment was directed toward me. My eyes shifted to Vicky. "I met Tammy already," she said in a low tone. "Her family moved into the house behind Knight's."

The old penny candy store? That place had been closed for years.

"Oh," I mouthed back, nodding.

Time travel sounded more plausible by the minute. *People seem to think I'm Mom.* Or maybe I looked so similar to her in seventh grade that they couldn't tell the difference.

There was one way to settle that question. Mom had a scar on her right shin from running into a barbed-wire fence when she was a kid. If it wasn't there, I was still me and just having a very strange morning.

Stealthily, I slid the cover from my Bic pen to the edge of my desk, then flicked it to the floor. Leaning over to pick it up, I grabbed the flared leg of my jeans and pulled it up slightly. My eyes widened, and my head started to pound.

Sister Cecilia clapped her hands together and motioned everyone to stand, turn to the American flag and put their hands over their hearts. After running my finger over the jagged scar, I followed the other kids' lead, stood up and mouthed the words to The Pledge of Allegiance since I didn't know it by heart.

"Does anyone have any prayer petitions?" Sister Cecilia asked. I had one. *I want my life back.* Didn't seem appropriate to share with the group, though.

"Pray for our dog, Duke." Edward Schultz, I noted, catching a glimpse of his nameplate. "He's getting old, and Pa's thinking of putting him down."

"Lord, hear our prayer." *Pa?* What was this, 1924? Turning my head to the left, I did a doubletake. A calendar was tacked to the bulletin board. Not 1924, but 1974. September 1974, to be precise.

Other petitions were put forward, something about someone's grandpa and the Vietnam War, but I couldn't take my eyes off the calendar. The chances of this being a prank got slimmer by the minute.

Calculating in my head, I realized that Mom would

have been thirteen that year. She'd have been a seventh-grader like I was. *Have I really been transported through time into her body?* If so, where was she?

Sister led the group in praying an Our Father, Hail Mary and the Glory Be to the Father prayer. I prayed along, asking God for insight so I could figure out what the heck was going on.

Prayers complete, Sister directed the first person in each row to grab a stack of literature books from the table to hand out to the students in their row.

For the time being, I would go with the flow. What other options were there anyhow? Other than having a complete freak-out, which had its considerations. I held myself in check. It probably wouldn't turn out too well for Mom when she got back into her body — which hopefully would be any minute now — if her classmates thought she was a complete lunatic.

Literature seemed to be the equivalent of English. When the bell rang at the end of class, Sister Cecilia left the room, and some of the kids got up to use the bathroom. The safest spot seemed to be my desk, so I stayed put, paging through the Literature book, feigning interest in the featured short stories.

"First day of school, already trying to be the teacher's pet?" Richard smirked at me. Ignoring the barb, I turned back to the book.

"You're going to be Sr. Cecilia's pet, all right. Her dog!"

I wasn't sure if I should respond to him or not. *Obviously, he thinks I'm Mom.* Was he just teasing her? They could be friends. With friends like that, who needs enemies?

Or, maybe he liked her? Guys sometimes did weird things when they were trying to get a girl's attention.

Thankfully, I didn't have to give it any more thought at that moment. The bell rang, kids scrambled back to their seats, and the next teacher walked in. My jaw dropped. Mr. Kovac? He'd been teaching at St. Joseph's forever. Other than his hair color, he looked just as he had on the last day of school three months ago.

A buzz ran through the room. Everyone was whispering. Maybe it was the mint green pants and the matching flowered shirt. Or, the white shoes. Definitely worth talking about. *That's a fashion statement if I've ever seen one.*

Mr. Kovac was Mrs. Baker's brother. The lady from the bank. I could picture her now, her name tag hanging around her thin neck. Gina Baker.

Holy cow! I never would've recognized her. Was that chunky kid with the kinky brown hair at the desk in front of Vicky really her? Yikes! Talk about a transformation.

"Howdy, kids."

The talking ceased abruptly.

"I'm your new teacher, Mr. Kovac. We're going to be learning about the exciting world around us through social studies."

An audible groan swelled up from the kids. Sounded as boring to them as it did to me.

Mr. Kovac plowed on. "Some of you may know me

because Gina's my kid sister."

I glanced over at the young Gina to gauge her reaction. Her eyes were downcast, and red crept from her neck to her forehead. Was this the first she'd heard of this?

"My wife and I have been married two years, and I'm happy to announce that we have a bun in the oven."

A few kids laughed. I turned to Vicky in confusion. She mouthed, "The rabbit died."

"What rabbit?" I asked.

Gina glared at me. "They're having a baby."

"Oh." Too much information.

"If you guys work hard learning social studies, it'll be swell for all of us."

Want to know what'd be really swell? Making it through this dumb day and getting my life back.

Chapter 9

It was somewhat confusing. We had Literature first hour and then Linguistics third hour. Maybe it was just me, but they both sounded like English classes. Mrs. Thompson clarified that her job as a Linguistics educator was to teach us the mechanics of writing. I didn't know there was such a thing. *Must not be that important since they don't teach it anymore.*

Apparently, there was a stockpile of sisters back in the day. Next hour, we had another one. Sister Joan taught music in the space across from the seventh-grade homeroom that was about the size of walk-in closet. There was enough room for an upright piano and three rows of risers, and that was it.

Another free-for-all ensued as kids grabbed spots on the risers. Like first hour, the boys gravitated to one side of the room and the girls to the other.

"Welcome to music class, children," Sister Joan said in a sing-song voice. "Time is of the essence. Need to determine your vocal range. One at a time, you'll step up to the piano, give me your name and sing the first two lines of America."

The reaction was immediate. A few people groaned, someone snorted, and one of the boys said, "No way, José." The less-than-enthusiastic response didn't deter Sr. Joan.

Immediately the girl in front of me shot her hand up. "I'll go first," she said. "If you want, I can do my own accompaniment. I've been playing the piano since I was three."

And Richard thought I was trying to be the teacher's pet?

"That's kind of you to offer..."

"Jane," she inserted.

"Jane, but I'll take care of that. Just focus on your singing."

"Yes, Sister," she dutifully replied.

Sister tapped the key for the first note. Jane confidently broke into song. Before the line was complete, Sister held her hand up. "Soprano." She scribbled a notation onto a sheet attached to a clipboard.

One after another, the girls filed up to the piano. Most sang well enough; Vicky struggled to stay on pitch. I was after her. My knees shook as I approached the piano.

The goal was to sing as quietly as possible. A few breathy words squeaked out of me.

"You can do better than that," urged Sister Joan. "Use your chest voice." Silence fell over the room. Snickers from the boys soon followed.

"What chest voice?"

Laughter erupted from the rest of the students. Warmth crept up my face. I narrowed my eyes at Richard.

"Again," said Sister Joan, hitting the first note. I increased my volume, keeping my eyes glued to the piano keys.

"Soprano," Sister said, grabbing her list. "Name?"

"Um, Allison Connors?"

"Next."

I went back to my spot on the risers and stared straight ahead. The queue dwindled until Richard was the only one left. He sauntered up to the piano, shoved his hands in his pockets, and when Sister started playing, he spoke the words of the song. I waited for Sister's reprimand.

The bell rang. "Bass," said Sr. Joan. "Pictures are next. Proceed to Sister Margaret Mary's office now."

That was it? Richard didn't have to humiliate himself like the rest of us? Lame. I rolled my eyes and followed the other kids down the steps to the first level. A line snaked into the library. The woman I assumed was Sister Margaret Mary sat behind a desk angled in the corner of the room. *Principal? Librarian? Hard to say.*

We were called up in alphabetical order. I was sandwiched between Matt Cavanaugh and Lawrence Coopman. They were quiet but seemed nice enough.

Stacy Ackerman was at the front of the line. The photographer handed her a black comb, told her to use it and pass it to the person behind her. Hasn't anyone here ever heard of lice? When Matt handed the comb to me, I passed it along to Lawrence, opting to comb my hair back with the headband instead. It wasn't like I'd ever see the picture anyhow.

"Individual shots first, then we'll line up for a group picture."

Obligingly, I smiled when it was my turn to take a seat on the swivel stool. I was a bit self-conscious, though. Mom's teeth went every which way but straight. Why hadn't Grandpa and Grandma taken her to an orthodontist? I'd been going to one since fourth grade.

Kids congregated at the back of the room after their pictures were taken. Vicky walked up to me, a puzzled look on her face.

"Where's your Lucky Locket Kiddles?"

I had no idea what she was talking about, so I shrugged my shoulders. Vicky held up the pendant hanging from a plastic chain around her neck. Other than a slightly different doll, it was identical to the necklace that was on Mom's dresser this morning.

Thinking on my feet, I blurted out, "I totally forgot."

"You forgot? We just talked about this last night when we were playing Kick the Can."

"We did? I mean, we did, but I'm having kind of a weird morning. It slipped my mind."

"Great," said Vicky. "We were going to be twins today, and now I look like a dweeb. I'm sure Mom's going to have something to say about this when she sees the picture."

"Sorry about that."

"Well, at least I found out before the group picture. I'll have to stash this somewhere before we line up. If Kurt sees it," she said, indicating the guy nearest the door, "he'll want it. Remember in fourth grade when he took that Avon bunny pin you wore for your picture and pinned it on his shirt for his individual picture?"

"Um, yeah."

"Man, he smelled like Sweet Honesty all afternoon

after he discovered there was perfume in there. Mrs. Bartol gave him strangest looks the rest of the day."

That actually did sound funny. I scanned the line to see what Kurt was up to now. Three guys clustered around him as he told a joke. When he delivered the punch line, there was dead silence. That didn't stop him from bursting out in laughter.

Vicky was right to want to hide the locket. That guy was strange.

Chapter 10

"Connie Ledoux, Patty Frederickson, Theresa Rogan, Allison Connors," yelled out Sister Margaret Mary, struggling to make herself heard over the din. "You may go to the cafeteria."

I had no idea why Mom got the special treatment, but I was good with it. The smell wafting up from the cafeteria made my stomach growl.

The four of us walked down to the school basement. Stepping into the hallway, it looked like it always had. Boys' bathroom, girls' bathroom, the large block room used as a gathering space, the cafeteria. The only thing missing were the double doors leading to the fieldhouse.

Steeping into the cafeteria, Connie and I were each handed a box by the lunch lady. "Dutch Masters, President," was printed on the top. Peeking inside, I counted two dollars in change.

"Thank you, Mrs. Gale," said Connie.

I parroted her response.

"Take positions on either side of the doorway," said Mrs. Gale. "Theresa, Patty, follow me."

Dutifully, I took the spot across from Connie. She was all smiles. Pumped about collecting lunch money?

"I'm excited about hot lunch..." Connie said enthusiastically. I eyed her skeptically. "This is my first time trying it!" My eyebrows shot up.

That explained the giddiness. I didn't want to burst her bubble, but hot lunch wasn't that amazing. I should know. I've had it every day since kindergarten. Her statement piqued my curiosity. Either she was the pickiest person on the planet or the poorest. According to the note inside the cigar box, lunch cost a whopping thirty-five cents. "Never?"

"You know," she said sheepishly, "with sixteen kids, it's cheaper to pack lunches. At least we get fresh-baked bread every morning."

My eyebrows shot up even higher. Sixteen? *Poorest, it is. Her mom must be a saint.*

Free lunch sounded pretty good for me today too. I didn't bring any money with me. How would I have known to do that? The system I was used to was automated.

Stampeding feet rumbled down the stairs, and we braced ourselves for the onslaught. Kids barreled to the doorway; money clutched tightly in their hands. We barely had a chance to catch our breath as the classes descended on us in waves.

Once the eighth-graders went through, we brought the money to the back of the kitchen, dumped it in a fake leather bank pouch, and then got our lunch trays.

"Goulash?" asked Mrs. Gale.

Never heard of it before, but it smelled tasty and looked edible.

"Sure," I replied.

I took a scoop of corn and two No-Bake Chocolate Cookies. They looked and smelled just like the ones

Mom makes. Thinking of her made me sigh. She should be living her first day of seventh grade, not me.

Not being able to resist, I took a nibble of a cookie. It didn't take long for the taste of the oatmeal, chocolate, peanut butter and sugar to ease me out of my funk.

The cafeteria was relatively quiet since the other kids were outside on the playground. The four of us girls ate at one of the deserted tables in the dining area. While we enjoyed our food, Patty, Theresa and Connie chatted about their summers. I listened, absorbing their stories.

After lunch, we hurried outdoors to catch the end of a soccer game. Sixth-, seventh- and eighth-grade girls were split between two teams on the grass field along the far edge of the school property. We divvied ourselves up between the two teams and got five minutes of playing time before the bell rang.

Each class lined up behind their homeroom teacher. The seventh-graders filed back upstairs to our classroom for math with another sister, Sister Martha. Class began with a math quiz that she corrected immediately. She separated the marked papers into piles and divided us into two groups.

I was assigned to the Robins and took a seat by the windows with the other kids in my group. The Bluebirds sat in desks on the other side of the room. You didn't have to be a math whiz to figure out that we were separated according to our abilities. Thankfully, I aced the quiz. It would suck if Mom came back to her life tomorrow and found herself in the dumb group because of me.

After Math, we went right into Science with, believe it or not, another sister. Sister Joachim. Ugh. Science. *My least favorite subject.* Regardless, I took meticulous notes so Mom would be able to slip right back into her life when she got here. *Any time now*, I thought, glancing around the room.

We had Sister Cecilia again in the afternoon for Religion. Our textbook was titled *Free to Live*, which we were encouraged to peruse. No boring Bible stories. That's different. Sister said it was meant to show how to be a Catholic in the modern world. My eyes fixed on a picture of a hippy holding a sign saying, "Give Peace A Chance." Not so sure about the "modern" part.

The last class of the day was Gym with the hip — or should I say hippy — Mr. Kovac. He went over various units he'd cover over the course of the school year, including one devoted to earning the President's Fitness Challenge. He held up the official certificate that kids would earn if they passed.

It read, "In recognition of outstanding physical achievement and exceptional dedication to the ideal of a sound mind in a strong body, my congratulations to you on this achievement." At the bottom it was signed, Richard Nixon. President of the United States.

There was no denying it. I had definitely landed smack dab in the middle of the '70s.

Chapter 11

When the last bell finally rang, I let out a drawn-out breath. Longest school day ever. Scrambling back to homeroom, we grabbed the clear bags and shoved our Math, Literature, Science and Social Studies books inside them.

Between the four books, they must've weighed ten pounds. Juggling the bag in my arms, I exited the classroom via the back set of stairs that led to the front of the building.

"Wait up!"

Vicky hustled to catch me on the steps.

"Hey, Vicky."

"Not too bad of a start today, huh?"

Easy for her to say. She hadn't woken up in someone else's body, been laughed at by a group of snotty girls for wearing the same shirt that one of them had on, or been humiliated by the class jock, twice at that.

"It was all right," I replied, shrugging my shoulders.

We exited the building side by side and made our way toward my house. That's right. Vicky's family used to live in our neighborhood. Technically, Grandma and Grandpa's neighborhood since they owned the house before Mom and Dad did.

As we strolled, we rehashed the day until we got to

the street that led to our house.

“See you tomorrow, Allison.”

“Sounds good.” *Not.* The last thing I wanted to do tomorrow was to see Vicky or anyone else from Mom’s seventh-grade class. I wanted to see my own classmates.

“I’ll call you later if I can,” she added.

“Great.” *Haven’t we covered everything already?*

Approaching our house, my pace slowed. I wasn’t sure what to expect when I got inside. Maybe it’d be like magic, and everything would be back to normal.

Fingers crossed, I stood at the bottom of the concrete back porch steps, a glimmer of hope running through me. The aroma drifting from the kitchen was unmistakable. Mom’s peanut butter brownies! I bounded up the steps two at a time and threw open the screen door.

Sure enough, there they were.

In Grandma’s hands. *Dang.*

As disappointing as it was to see Grandma, that didn’t stop me from grabbing a brownie. I inhaled that sweet goodness. The scent was slightly different from Mom’s, but one bite and I was sold. These were the softest brownies I’d ever tasted.

“How was the first day of school?”

“Fine,” I mumbled around the mouthful of brownie.

Grandma eyed me expectantly. After an awkward moment of silence, she tried a different tactic.

“Any homework?”

“We have to cover our books,” I replied, dropping

the book bag on the kitchen table with a thud.

"There's plenty of paper bags in the back closet."

And you're telling me that, why? Math whiz that I was, I put two and two together a moment later. *For covering the books. Got it.*

"Cool."

After downing the rest of the brownie, I stepped into the walk-in closet. Bags, check.

"Where are the tape and scissors?"

The water in the kitchen stopped running. "Should be in the phone bench where they always are."

Phone bench. That must be what they call that desk thing in the front entryway.

No scissors or tape in the top drawer, but I did find something interesting. City Directory. Flipping through the pages, I looked up Grandma and Grandpa.

Connors, Michael, 205 Washington St., 3-3019. Five digits? Was that their whole phone number?

Locating the tape and scissors in the second drawer, I nearly jumped out of my skin when the phone near my head rang. *Holy crap*, that was loud.

Grandma didn't make a move towards the entryway, so I tentatively picked up the handpiece.

"Hello?"

Before the person on the other end could utter a word, Grandma piped up from the kitchen. "Connors, Ally speaking!"

Swiveling my head in her direction, I saw her raised eyebrows. I turned back to the phone.

"Connors, um... Ally speaking?"

"Hey, Allison, it's Vicky."

"Oh, hey."

"Crissy has a doctor's appointment. Dad just came and picked Mom and her up, so I can talk for a little bit."

Crissy... That must have been one of Vicky's little sisters. Could be the one with the heart issues. Her dad? I swore that Mom said Mr. Holtz died when she and Vicky were seniors in high school. *This is starting to get freaky!*

For the next twenty minutes, Vicky rambled on, and I listened half-heartedly. My ears perked up when the subject of Mr. Kovac came up.

"Mr. Kovac is nice and everything, but he's trying too hard to be cool," noted Vicky. "The boys think he's the best thing since sliced bread, but if he doesn't chill out, this is going to get super annoying."

Hasn't bread always been sliced?

After enough time perched on the wooden phone bench, I tested to see if the curly phone cord was long enough to get out of earshot of Grandma. She putzed around the kitchen, no doubt listening to every word of our conversation.

Couldn't get any further than the den. So much for that. By now, the phone was so warm it was burning my ear. And they say cell phones are bad for your health.

"Hey, Vicky, gotta go. My mom needs something."

"That's fine. I'll see you at my house in the morning. Quarter-to-eight?"

"Sure. See you then."

I hung the phone up, grabbed my books off the kitchen table and started the trek through the dining room and family room to get to the stairs.

"What exactly do I need, Ally?"

Busted. I sheepishly pivoted to address Grandma, who was sitting in the chair Mom usually occupied at the dining room table. One glance, and I froze.

A cigarette dangled from her lips. Lit. Inside the house.

Maybe Grandma was the one with a head injury. She hadn't smoked since before I was born.

"What the heck are you doing?"

She took a drag and stamped out the cigarette in a gold ashtray.

"That's what I was going to ask you."

My eyes as big as saucers, I backed slowly away from her. Making it to the family room, I took off for the stairs, streaking up to the second floor. Racing down the hall, I stumbled into my room and slammed the door shut behind me.

Get me the heck out of here!

Chapter 12

Safe from the smoke, I threw the bookbag on the floor and flopped onto the bed. Scenes from the day looped through my head. Try as I might, I still couldn't figure out what was going on.

After a while, I'd had enough and sat up. With nothing better to do, I grabbed the book-covering supplies. A plastic box with a ridged knob on its side caught my attention. Was that a radio? Turning the knob, the final notes of a song faded out.

"You're listening to WWKA, today's top hits. This is William Rogan spinning cool songs for cool cats. Request lines are open."

There was a Theresa Rogan in Mom's class. Were they related? The next song started. I listened as I configured the grocery bag into a book cover.

"Billy, don't be a hero, don't be a fool with your life. Billy, don't be a hero, come back and make me your wife." The song was as hokey as the DJ.

Twenty minutes later, the project was complete. Bored with the music, I meandered downstairs. Grandma's chair was deserted, but voices came from the kitchen. One of those guys must be home from school.

A small-screen TV was set into a cabinet on the den floor. No remote control in sight, I walked up to it and pulled the On/Off knob. It took a good thirty seconds for the screen to be fully lit. There were three channels to choose from. I clicked on Channel 2. *The Brady Bunch.* That was one of Mom's favorite shows when she was a kid.

As the opening song played, I took a seat in the recliner by the arched doorway.

No sooner had I settled in, the young Uncle Robert stepped into the room and positioned himself in front of the TV.

"What's up, shrimp?" he asked, putting his hands on his hips to completely block my view.

"Nothing," I said, leaning over to look past him. "Can you get out of the way? The show's starting."

"The Brady Boogers? Haven't you seen that a thousand times?

First time actually. Trying to think like Mom would, I shot back, "So what if I did?"

"*Wild Wild West* is a hundred times better." Robert bent down and changed the channel.

I couldn't let him get away with this. The first word that occurred to me sprang to my lips. "Mo-o-om!"

"You kids, stop fighting." The oven door slammed shut. Robert didn't budge.

After the crappy day I had, this was the last straw. Bolting out of the chair, I pulled him away from the set. "Move it! I was here first."

"No, you weren't. I watched *Gilligan's Island.* I was coming right back."

"Like heck you were. The TV was off when I got here."

He didn't budge.

"Mo-o-om! Make him get out of my way!"

"Robert Dean, stop picking on your sister."

"Baby," said Robert, giving me a shove. "All you have to do is whine, and Mom gives you anything you want."

"Whatever."

Robert threw one last snotty look at me and stalked out of the room.

Did Mom have to put up with this crap all the time?

Dismissing him from my mind, I changed the channel back and resumed watching the show. The Brady kids said things like "far out" and "groovy." I'd spent the entire day living in the 1970s and hadn't heard either of those. Maybe it was a California thing.

After the show, Grandma called from the other room.

"Ally, can you come here once?"

Come here once? That must be where Mom got that expression.

"I need you to set the table."

"Sure." I turned the TV off and walked into the kitchen. The plates were in their normal spot. Grabbing five, I set the table like I normally would for Mom, Dad, me and the boys. *As much as they all drove me crazy, I'd give anything to see them right now.*

Through the bank of kitchen windows, I saw the green car from this morning pull back into the driveway. So, that really *was* Grandpa.

Stepping outside, I spoke up when he got out of the car. "Hi, Dad."

No adverse reaction, so I plowed on. "How was the base today?"

"Same old, same old. How was school?"

"All right."

"Ally, get the boys for supper," Grandma called from the kitchen.

Stepping back into the kitchen, I went out on a limb and yelled for the boys using Grandma's nicknames for them. "Howie! Robbie!"

"Ally! I could have done that myself. Go upstairs and get them."

Not wanting to get Mom in trouble, I did as I was told. When I got to the bottom landing, I shouted up the stairs, "Time for dinner!"

The boys came out of their rooms. "Dinner!" mocked Robert as he flew down the steps. "Is that what the *Brady Boogers* call it?"

Isn't that what everyone calls the last meal of the day?

Howard brushed past me. "Get out of my way, twerp!"

What's up with these two? Hard to imagine they'd ever found anyone willing to marry them. My poor aunts.

Chapter 13

Meatloaf, corn, boiled potatoes. *Mom's life, my life; at the moment, I didn't care.* I loved Grandma's cooking and couldn't wait to dig in.

Following Grandpa's lead, the boys and I made the sign of the cross and did the *Bless Us O Lord* prayer.

"Good food, good meat, good God, let's eat," added Robert, before stabbing his fork into a piece of meatloaf.

"Robbie," Grandma scolded. He shrugged and reached out for the potatoes. With the food dished, Grandpa had each of us kids say something about our day.

Howard, three grades older than Mom, announced that they'd posted the roles for *The Fantasticks* that he'd tried out for last week. He'd gotten the lead role. Apparently, that was a big deal since he was only a sophomore. He then ran through his class schedule. All college prep classes plus Art. Second-quarter, he'd start driver's ed.

It was surprising that he and Robert didn't seem to get along. It sounded like they had a lot in common. Robert's daily schedule was similar to Howard's, except instead of Art, he had men's chorus. Nine months younger than Howard, Robert would do driver's ed fourth quarter.

Next, it was my turn. Dutifully, I listed off each class and who taught them.

"Think this will be the year you beat Theresa for the top spot in your class?" Grandpa asked.

Is that a thing in seventh grade? Did it really matter?

"I don't know."

"Stay one step ahead of her, and you'll be positioned to win the Maxwell Award next year, like your brother."

I glanced between Howard, who had a smug expression on his face, and Robert, who rolled his eyes. It was obvious who'd earned it. Talk about competition; no wonder these two weren't the best of friends.

"Anything else?" Grandpa asked.

"That's about it."

"Mike," Grandma piped in. "If you really want to hear the full scoop, just listen the next time the phone rings. If it's Vicky, you'll hear every detail of Ally's life."

Now it was my turn to roll my eyes. *Really, Grandma?* You must have annoyed the crap out of Mom when she was my age.

After dinner, supper, whatever, the guys scattered, leaving me and Grandma alone in the kitchen. She ran hot water into the sink, squirted dish soap in, set the dishes in the soapy water and handed a towel to me.

Guess that means I'm the official dish dryer.

"Thanks, Ally," she said as she finished rinsing the pots and pans. "I can finish drying if you want to run over to Wendy's to see how her first day of school went."

Not really. Would it seem out of character for Mom if I didn't?

Other than being next-door neighbors, I don't think Mom and Wendy Olson were ever close. They were completely opposite personalities, at least as adults. But, anything to pass the time. I just wanted to get this day over so I could go to bed, wake up and get back to my own life.

Chapter 14

The door opened before I even had a chance to knock.

"Hey, Ally."

"Hi, uh, Wendy." The girl standing before me had thick, wavy, dishwater blond hair halfway down her back and wore metal-rimmed octagonal-shaped glasses.

No offense, Mom, but this chick is much cooler than you were at this age.

"Wanna hang out on the front porch?"

I nodded and followed her through the side yard to the front of their house.

"Hopefully, Wayne didn't see us. He's been following me around for the last two hours."

Must be her little brother. I could relate. Brock and Brayden drove me up a tree too.

"Mom had to put up with him all afternoon. I'm sure she's counting down the days until he's in first grade next year."

I nodded in commiseration.

"How was your first day of school?"

"Not much different than fifth grade at Faith Lutheran. Our new teacher rags on us just as much as Mrs. B. did last year."

She attended Faith Lutheran? You'd never know it

by the life that she led now.

Wanting to change subjects, I asked if she'd watched *The Brady Bunch* after school.

"Heck, yah. Greg is fine. He's the only reason I watch that dumb show."

"Yah, he's fine," I agreed, copying her lingo. "Peter's not so bad, either."

"Are you kidding me? He's as femmy as Mr. Brady."

So much for that conversation. It trailed off until Wendy piped up with an idea.

"How about we get some kids together to play night games?"

Night games? "Um, okay."

"Get your brothers. I'll get Scott."

Henderson? The sheriff's deputy? Wonder what he looked like as a kid. It'd be weird seeing him with hair; he didn't have much of it now.

As directed, I went back to our house and talked to Howard and Robert. Surprisingly, they were amenable to playing. Robert even offered to run through the backyard to see if Julie Jacobs wanted to join us.

It was a yes for Scott. Wendy dragged me one more house down to the Thorps'. Wasn't sure how many kids they had, but three teenagers poked their head out of a battered, psychedelic bus parked in their driveway. They were in.

In total, eleven kids gathered in front of our corner lot. After a little back and forth, the group decided to start the night off playing *Seven Steps Around the House.*

Took about five seconds to figure out how to play the game but about five minutes to diffuse each argument that ensued. Whoever was "it" always said they saw people moving, and the people who weren't "it" always swore they weren't.

After about the tenth argument, the call was made to switch to *Kick the Can*, allegedly Mom's favorite game when she was a kid. My heart raced when we started. I took off running with all the rest of the kids while Janice Thorp counted to fifteen. Once I rounded the corner of the house, I dove into the bushes and waited a couple of minutes, noting as other kids got caught.

When Janice walked past the bushes and didn't see me, it was the ideal opportunity to make my break for the front yard. Hearing the noise coming from the bushes, she turned around and sprinted after me. Fortunately, I was able to kick the empty can before Janice could put her foot on it.

For one shining moment, I felt like a hero.

We played for another half-hour. When the streetlights came on, people drifted home. It was 8:30 when we got into the house. Not sure what else to do, I went upstairs, grabbed my Laura Ingalls Wilder-style nightgown and went downstairs to take a shower.

Being in that familiar shower, it was easy to imagine that everything was back to normal. After fifteen minutes, I reluctantly turned off the water. With my hair dripping wet, I searched the cupboard for the blow dryer. Nothing.

No big deal if I went to bed with my hair wet.

Tomorrow morning, everything is going to be back to normal. I just know it. Nothing I did today would even matter anymore.

With a few minutes to spare before bedtime, I took a seat on the couch next to Grandpa's recliner. He was watching the Yankees game. The game held no interest for me, but he did. I wanted to burn the image of the young Grandpa into my memory banks. He really was good-looking back in the day.

A clock in another room chimed nine times.

"Good night... Dad."

"Good night, Allison," he replied, eyes still glued to the TV.

Upstairs, I knocked on the bedroom door next to the bathroom.

"Come in."

I stepped in and did a doubletake. Grandma was reading in bed. A twin bed. Next to it was another twin bed. It looked like a scene from *I Love Lucy*.

"Goodnight... Mom." It still felt odd calling her that.

She set the *McCall's* magazine down. "Goodnight, Ally. Sleep tight."

"Thanks. You too."

The boys' bedroom doors were closed. A Paul McCartney and Wings song came from Robert's bedroom, with him playing the guitar in accompaniment. *Wow, he's pretty good.*

No sound came from Howard's room, but the lights were on, so he was probably studying his lines or doing homework.

"Good night, Uncle Howard. Good night, Uncle Robert. It was nice getting to know the younger you," I whispered before tiptoeing down the hall to my room.

I crawled into bed, turned off the lamp and started my prayers.

Thank you, God, for getting me through this day.

A sigh escaped my lips. Spending time in Mom's growing-up world had been interesting, that's for sure. But it was temporary. *When I wake up tomorrow morning, it'll be time to live my own life again.*

Chapter 15

The sound of ticking gradually woke me. Keeping my eyes closed, I lay still and listened for a few seconds, hope diminishing with each tick. I forced my eyes open. The little wind-up clock stared me in the face.

This was not what I'd anticipated. I took in a few deeps breaths to keep from losing it. *God, why am I still here?*

Maybe He was teaching me a lesson. Maybe I should've been more appreciative of how lucky and blessed my life was. I lived in a nice house, we were in a safe town, Mom and Dad loved each other and us kids, Brock and Brayden were okay brothers, I went to a good school, and for the most part, I had solid friendships.

This left me with some serious thinking to do. One by one, I ticked off the events that happened over the previous day and a half.

1) Last normal experience = volleyball practice Sunday night. 2) Got a pretty good knock to my head when Hailey plowed me over. 3) Went to bed that night = other than the goose egg, everything seemed fine. 4) Woke up yesterday = same house but different surroundings. 5) Grandpa, Grandma, Uncle Howard, Uncle Robert = younger versions of the people I know. 6) Mom, Dad, Brock, Brayden = missing.

I paused and looked up to the left. 7) No one seems

to think anything is out of the normal except me. 8) Town looks the same for the most part. 9) St. Joseph's is the same school but no fieldhouse. 10) Sisters teach there. 11) Some of the kids in Mom's class I know as adults because they still live in town.

And the kicker. 15) Morgan = Allison. Everyone I encountered yesterday thought that I was seventh-grade Mom. Which I could understand, seeing that I had apparently taken up residence in her body. That's just a weird thought.

Maybe I'd been abducted by aliens and was living in a simulation on another planet. Or, even worse, maybe I was still living on Earth, but everyone else had been abducted.

Not wanting to consider that possibility, I rolled out of bed. With the thought that I should do something that felt normal, I made the bed, snapped open the funky white shade, and walked into the closet to pick out clothes for school.

Was it just that one shirt, or did that Rebecca girl and Mom have more matching clothes? *Not going to be the ugly twin today.* She didn't seem to be the camping type. I grabbed the Camp Red Rocks t-shirt and the groovy brown bell-bottom cords.

Dressed, I slowly descended the stairs, not sure what to expect. No surprise, the retro '70s vibe was still hanging around. That and the smell of cigarette smoke. *Ugh.*

The first floor was empty. From the dining room, I could see the open garage door. *Grandpa must've left for work already.* Footsteps lumbering down the steps caused me to jump. I braced myself for my first encounter of the day with Howard and Robert.

They whisked by me on their way to the kitchen without saying a word. After stepping into the back closet, they came out with their schoolbooks and headed out the back door.

"Good morning to you too," I said sarcastically.

The screen door creaked back open. I waited expectantly.

"Ma said to start her coffee," Robert said. "She's getting up in a few minutes."

Was he talking to me? Instinctively, I looked behind my shoulder. No one there.

"Uh, sure."

No Keurig sitting on the countertop. How did people make coffee back in the Stone Age? I dug through the cabinets, searching for clues. Folgers Coffee. Check. Metal coffee pot with cord. Check. Following the directions on the back of the metal can, I scooped coffee grinds into the basket inside the coffee pot, filled the container with water, and plugged the pot in. Immediately the thing started making hiccoughing noises. It must be doing something.

Pink Panther Flakes, the cereal choice of the day. *If that doesn't say nutrition, I don't know what does.* The scent of coffee soon filled the air. *Booyah!* Rocking the '70s now! With the last of the milk drained from my cereal bowl, I ran upstairs to brush my teeth.

It didn't seem possible that I was going into day two of Mom's life. As I walked to Vicky's, I kept my eye out for lightning. Who knew what it'd take to zap me back to the present.

Vicky was still scrambling around her kitchen when I got there. She hadn't even covered her books. With my new-found book-covering skills, we were able to knock that project out in less than five minutes.

"We should take our bikes to school sometime," said Vicky. "We'd get there faster."

Or, you could actually be ready on time.

The image of Mom's banana-seat bike I'd spied in the garage came to mind. *Not going to happen on my watch.* As if the chunky tires weren't dorky enough, she had to go and add an orange pole and flag to the back of the bike. That really made it a show stopper. No wonder the boys in Mom's class picked on her.

Despite wearing braces and glasses — albeit more fashionable frames than Mom's — Vicky seemed pretty cool. She was super chill, had hip clothes, and was nice to everyone from what I saw yesterday. I could see why Mom liked her.

Vicky sat down to tie her shoes. I glanced at the clock above their refrigerator. Five to eight? *How'd it get so late?*

"Mrs. Holtz, is that the right time?" I asked Vicky's mom, my voice rising.

She didn't even bother to look away from the dish she was rinsing to answer. "Ten minutes ahead."

That was a relief. Was it purposely set like that?

"Bye, Mom, Bye, Crissy," Vicky said, opening the back door.

"Bye, bye, Vicky," came a tiny voice from around

the corner. A little girl tiptoed into the kitchen and hugged Vicky around the knees.

Oh my gosh, that must be the sister with the heart issues. She was adorable! With her wispy blond hair, China-blue eyes and pale skin, she looked like a porcelain doll. The only imperfections were her blue-tipped fingers and blue-tinted lips.

Vicky scooped Crissy up in a hug. "See you after school, munchkin!"

As much as I wanted to give her a squeeze too, we had to fly. We got to school with two minutes to spare. Bolting up the back steps to the auditorium, we made it to our seats a moment before the bell rang.

The day started out just as the previous day had – Pledge of Allegiance, prayers, announcements. Sr. Cecilia spelled out the schedule for the day. Instead of Religion and Gym for our last two classes, both the boys and the girls would be walking over to the high school for Home Economics. *Cooking and sewing classes? With boys? It'd almost be worth sticking around for a while just to see that. Almost. I'm still taking the first train back to Normalville.*

The morning passed quickly. One memorable moment. Vicky went up to talk to Mr. Kovac as he stood next to this overhead projector machine. He was organizing slides in the dim light.

As Vicky neared the front of the room, she readjusted her glasses with one hand while balancing her Social Studies book in the other hand. She mustn't have noticed the projector cord in the aisle and tripped over it. The book slipped, and — in an attempt to grab it before it fell to the floor — she ripped a page right out of it.

Like the rest of the kids in the class, I burst out laughing. Vicky glared at me when she came back to her seat. Busted. *Hope that doesn't affect your friendship with Vicky long-term, Mom.*

Chapter 16

I got the cold shoulder from Vicky during Math. She'd walked by me without saying a word on her way to the Bluebird side of the room. At lunchtime, she stood in Connie's line to pay for her lunch instead of mine.

It bugged me, but I got over it when I saw the fresh-baked gooey chocolate-frosted brownies for dessert. After Connie, Theresa, Patty and I ate, we ran out to the soccer field. I gave Vicky space and put myself on the other team.

Science dragged on forever. I wasn't the only one getting antsy. As soon as the bell rang, we flipped open the tops of our desks, grabbed our book bags, shoved homework in them, and sprang from our seats. Streaming towards the staircase at the back of the auditorium, we bolted down the steps and out the building.

I caught up with Vicky on the blacktop before we crossed the street.

"Sorry about laughing at you before."

"That's okay," she said with a sigh. "It wasn't that big of a deal. I just can't get used to these stupid glasses."

"I totally know what you mean," I said, pushing my nerdy plastic glasses up. "Wanna walk with me to the high school?"

"Sure."

The boys were ahead of us. After crossing the bridge spanning Beaver Brook, Richard turned back and glowered at me and Vicky. "We're being followed by a dog," he said, elbowing Greg Kohler in the side.

I pivoted and glanced over my shoulder. I didn't see any dog. Swinging back, Richard looked directly at me.

"I was talking about you, sheepdog." I stopped dead in my tracks. My mind scrambled for a great comeback, but nothing came to me. Give me a half-hour, and I'd probably come up with the ideal thing to say, but that wouldn't help now.

Richard turned away and started barking. A few boys around him followed his lead.

"Don't worry about him. He's a big jerk," said Vicky.

"You can say that again," I replied, doing my best to sound calm. Inside I was cringing. *How many kids heard him?*

We slowed down and let the other girls pass us. I wanted as much space between me and Richard as possible. Vicky was right. He was a jerk. A colossal jerk.

After we got to the high school, we found the home economics room. Mrs. Wojcik was very enthusiastic about cooking and sewing. The first semester, the seventh-graders would be in the big kitchen every Tuesday, learning to make breakfast foods. On Thursdays, the class would be in the adjoining room sewing.

The whole hour, the boys were grouped on one side of the room with the girls on the other side, so I didn't have to worry about being near Richard. When the bell rang, the country kids took the hallway to the left to get to the parking lot where the busses were parked. The city kids went the opposite way to head out through the double doors on the north side of the building.

Vicky and I crossed High Street and walked toward her dad's business. I recognized the building, but I hadn't known it as Holtz's Flooring. It was one of those dollar stores now.

The building next door was a gas station. That hadn't changed.

"My mom gave me twenty cents yesterday for watching Charles and Sherry. That's enough for two pops. Want one?"

Assuming she meant soda, I was all in. "Sure!"

A small bell attached to the glass door chimed as we stepped into the building. "Woah," said Vicky, "A pop machine with cans instead of bottles? Cool!"

"Yah, cool," I echoed. These people were easily impressed.

"I'm getting a Dr. Pepper," she said, "What do you want?"

"I'll take that one," I said, pointing to the Tahitian Treat label. *Might as well try something new while I'm here.*

Sodas in hand, we crossed the parking lot to her dad's store.

"Hi, Allison," said Mr. Holtz in a cheery voice. He put his arm around Vicky's shoulder. "Hi, honey." She didn't look too enthusiastic about the PDA.

Mr. Holtz's brown eyes showed concern. Was there a chance that he'd already been diagnosed with his cancer?

Knowing what the future held for the people was kind of creepy. No time to dwell on that because Vicky set her soda down on her dad's desk, kicked her shoes off, and said, "Race you!"

She took off like a shot, and instinctively, I flipped off my shoes and bolted off behind her. We jumped from roll to roll, one end of the long building to the other. After fifteen minutes, we were sweating up a storm. The sodas were gulped down in a minute flat.

We said our goodbyes to Mr. Holtz and started the trek home. At the alley, I turned left to take the shortcut to our house. I wanted to get my homework done before *The Brady Bunch* came on.

"I'll call you after supper if I can," said Vicky. "I have to babysit all the kids tonight, so it might be a little later. They have to be in bed first. Otherwise, Charles will nark on me. He's such a tattletale."

Tell me about it. Just imagine having two of the little rugrats like I do.

"Sounds good. Talk to you later."

Or not. At some point, I have to get off this crazy carousel, right?

Chapter 17

By chance, Howard was in the alley when I stepped in. For a moment, I observed him as he walked.

It was still hard to believe that this kid would grow up to be the fun-loving Uncle Howard that I knew. He was kind of a crank now.

Who knows, maybe I'd judged him too quickly. I quickened my pace to catch up. Hearing my footsteps, he glanced back. Seeing that it was me, he resumed walking. At least he didn't speed up. Taking that as a good sign.

"Hi," I said.

"Hey," he replied.

"Don't you have play practice today?"

"They're working on a scene I'm not in. Besides, I have to study for my ACT test. Dad expects me to ace it, so I get that appointment to West Point."

He didn't seem too excited about that prospect. Was Grandpa pressuring him to join the military? Thinking back to Dad signing me up for the PSATs, I realized that nothing has changed in that regard. Parents, at least in our family, always have high expectations for their kids no matter what era they live in.

Maybe that's why he's so grouchy. He's probably got a lot on his mind. We walked the rest of the way home in silence. Once we got there and had dumped our stuff in the back closet, I made a beeline to the bread drawer to get a snack.

Howard walked out of the closet and saw me, brownie in hand.

“Where’d you get that?”

“Mom had the leftovers wrapped in aluminum foil in the bread drawer.”

“You mean tin foil?”

“Um... totally what I meant. Studying elements in science today. Just got a little mixed up.”

“Right.”

I grabbed my bookbag and ran upstairs to get changed and start my homework. Literature was easy, but I got stumped on some of the Math problems. Hearing water running in the bathroom sink, I wondered if Grandpa was home. Maybe he could help me.

Sure enough, I walked to the bathroom and saw him running a razor over his shaving-cream slathered chin.

“Dad,” I said tentatively, still getting used to the new title. “Can you help me with Math?”

“Just a minute.”

I watched as he continued his routine. He rubbed V-05 between his palms and ran his fingers through his hair, combed it down and then patted English Leather aftershave on his cheeks.

Approving the final outcome, he grabbed the book that I held out to him, stepped into his and Grandma’s bedroom and took a seat on the bed nearest the window.

"Which one?"

"Can you look over the first couple?" I asked, pointing to my notebook. "We're just learning to divide decimals. I want to make sure I'm doing this right, but I don't have a calculator to check."

"A calculator? Does anyone in your class have one?"

Come to think of it, I hadn't noticed any.

"I'm not sure."

"I can get my slide rule, if that'll help."

How would a ruler solve a multiplying problem? "That's okay. Can you just do a quick check?"

Pencil in hand, Grandpa looked over my calculations while I looked him over. He was a cool guy back then. Tall, thin, kind of resembled JFK.

"Looks good to me."

"Thanks, Dad."

"You're welcome. Need to get to work now. Have a good night."

Work? Hadn't he just gotten home from the base? I dug through my memory banks. *That's right,* he used to have a second job tending bar at River's Edge Golf Course & Supper Club.

"You too." I jumped off the bed and flung my arms around his waist. Grandpa patted my shoulder and then broke away to snatch his keys from the dresser.

Since Grandpa would be eating at work, Grandma whipped up a casual meal for the rest of us. Hot dogs and these things called Potato Stix. Greasy and salty fake French fries from a can. Side dishes don't get much better than that.

Howard and Robert scarfed down three hot dogs each and cleaned out the Potato Stix can. It was amazing how thin they were. Would it break time-travel protocol if I told them that one day their metabolism would come to a screeching halt? Those poor eating habits were going to catch up with them.

With school in full swing, it sounded like night games were over for the year. After Grandma and I finished the dishes, everyone took their spots in the den for a night of TV watching. Not feeling inclined to squash myself between Howard and Robert, I perched on the glider rocker. They all seemed into the shows, but I was more intrigued by the old-school commercials. They were so hokey.

When I went to bed, I lay wide awake, thinking over everything that had happened in the last twenty-four hours. It wasn't easy jumping into somebody's life, not knowing what the dynamics were between them and the other people surrounding them.

Had there been bad blood between Mom and Richard before I got here? If he was going to act this way all seventh grade, I felt sorry for her. Fingers and toes crossed, I hoped this was my last day dealing with him. I was more than ready to put the ball back in Mom's court.

Chapter 18

Groundhog Day, take three.

Following the morning routine that I'd established, I got up, made my bed, picked out clothes from the lame selection in Mom's closet, got dressed, went downstairs, started Grandma's coffee, and ate a bowl of sugar-coated cold cereal.

Steering clear of the boys, I waved to Grandpa when he pulled out of the garage, brushed my teeth, grabbed the nifty bookbag, and headed out the back door to walk to Vicky's.

"Bye, Mom," I yelled as I stepped over the threshold.

"Bye, Ally," came her voice from the second floor. "Have fun at Scouts today."

Scouts? Crap! I raced back to my bedroom and grabbed the Girl Scout sash I'd seen in Mom's closet. *Scout manual?* Sweeping through everything on the bottom shelf, I snared the book, then raced back down the steps and flew out the screen door.

Vicky was actually waiting for me on her concrete back porch when I got to their yard. Spotting the sash in my bookbag, I heard her say, "Shoot," and then head back into her house. A minute later, she reappeared, sash and manual clutched in her hand.

With a friend like Vicky, I could see why Mom was such a skinny kid. No such thing as a leisurely walk to school with that chick. We skidded into our desks just in time to begin the Wednesday routine.

Looking around me, I noticed everyone wearing their Girl Scout sashes, so I took Mom's sash out of her book bag and put it on too.

On Wednesdays, we had Art instead of Music. Balancing the jumbo box of sixty-four crayons, a pair of pointy silver scissors and Elmer's glue in one arm, I stepped into the queue and followed the rest of the class downstairs.

Walking into the room, I spotted Sister Cecilia. Literature and Art, quite the diverse resume.

I half-listened as she went through the agenda for the year, something about working on Art projects that aligned with the various seasons, blah, blah, blah... Mom could figure it out when she got back. At least the room was big enough to put a decent amount of space between me and Richard. There was a chance that his behavior the last two days was out of character for him, but I'd give him a wide berth either way.

Sister handed us letter-sized pieces of white paper and told us to draw out our last names using pictures. Miller would have been easy. Even I can draw a can of beer. But Connors?

I looked around to see what other people came up with. There were some artistic kids in the class. In less than five minutes, Bobbi Jo Howell had sketched an authentic-looking American Indian, right arm bent at the elbow, palm facing forward with the word "How" written in a balloon above his head. Next to that, she put a plus sign and a three-dimensional L.

With time winding down, I ended up writing the word Connors in balloon letters, colored in various shades using an assortment of my sixty-four crayons. Each one was meticulously sharpened before I repositioned it in the box.

As we gathered our supplies to take back to homeroom, something slid off the art table on the other side of the room. The sound made everyone look.

A box of crayons, thankfully not as big as mine, lay on the floor, crayons scattered everywhere. They were Richard's. He saw me glance his way.

"Fetch," he commanded.

My eyes widened, but I didn't move.

"I was talking to you," he said. He wadded up his artwork and threw it at my shoulder. My eyes narrowed as I glared at him.

"Ruff, ruff," he said, low enough that Sister couldn't hear but loud enough that some of the kids nearby did. A flush ran up my face. I looked around at the other kids. Everyone seemed to be hyper-focused on packing up their supplies.

Just then, it hit me. I could see what the deal was. No one wanted to be Richard's next target. Not that I blamed them. He was taller than just about everybody in class and a lot more muscular. If the situation were happening to someone else in class, I wouldn't have the guts to stand up to him either.

The bell rang. I was more than ready to go back upstairs to Math and sit by the smart kids and get away from that idiot, Richard.

Chapter 19

There was a bit of excitement on the soccer field during recess. Us girls working in the lunchroom saw the commotion when we got out there after lunch. Brenda Gale lay on her side, right bent leg held up to her chest. The other girls swarmed around her.

A fifth-grader perched in the climbing tower gave us the scoop. According to her, play had been getting intense, and one of the eighth-graders took Brenda out with a nasty kick to her ankle.

A priest stormed over from the football field.

"Father Laroche doesn't look happy," said Patty.

"If I've told you, girls, once, I've told you a thousand times, cut out the rough play," he shouted as he stepped onto the soccer field. "You're worse than the boys." He looked from face to face. "Someone owes Brenda an apology."

Crickets.

"God knows the truth," said Father in a guilt-inducing tone. Still not a sound. "I better see each one of you in confession Saturday."

As a group, they answered, "Yes, Father." *They were all going to confession? I find that hard to believe.*

Father put one hand under Brenda's knees and one behind her shoulders and scooped her off the ground. Straightening up, he headed to the school building. I was glad that I wasn't involved. That lecture was brutal.

When we got back to homeroom, Brenda was at her desk with her bad leg propped up on a folding chair. The boys were impressed with the nice bruises she sported.

Lucky for her, we had Science and Religion back to back, so she didn't have to get out of her seat. After Mrs. Gale finished her shift in the cafeteria, she came and helped Brenda hobble out of the room so she could go home early.

When the final bell rang, the scouts headed down to the gym room for the meeting. Every girl in Mom's class was in scouting except Sheila, who had a bus to catch, and Gina, who lived in town but, for whatever reason, wasn't in the troop.

Monica Caruso's mom was the main scout leader, and Angela Bergner's mom was the co-leader. Mrs. Rogan would help during the weeks that she was on first shift at the hospital.

Mrs. Caruso went through her spiel, welcoming Tammy Obermeier to scouting, making announcements and laying out the agenda for the year. With no intention of being in this troop for more than ninety minutes, I tuned out.

My ears perked up when I heard the word snack. Chocolate chip cookies provided by Laura Mueller's mom? Score! After devouring every cookie on the tray, girls were called up one at a time and awarded badges that they'd earned over the summer.

Mom has been a busy girl. Six badges altogether. I inspected the stitched pictures, trying to guess what they were for.

The meeting concluded with a vote between going to winter camp or spring camp. Winter camp would be indoors at Camp Red Rock's lodge. Spring camp would be outdoors in platform tents.

This one's for you, Mom. I threw my hand up and voted for the first option. Didn't matter how cold it got, camping indoors was better than camping outdoors any day. Mom's side won the vote. Winter camp, it would be.

After the meeting, Vicky, Connie, Tammy and I walked home together as far as South Elementary. From there, Connie continued straight to her street, and the rest of us turned right to walk the last couple blocks to our houses. It was the first time Tammy had come with us. Normally she had to accompany her little sister Tina to school and back.

It was almost five o'clock, and I smelled dinner cooking as I approached the stoop. Meandering into the kitchen, I pulled the top off the pan on the stove. Horseshoe-shaped meat. Hopefully, it tasted better than it looked.

By the time I put my school stuff away, everyone was seated at the kitchen table. The mystery meat was ring bologna. Smothered in ketchup, it was pretty good. Of course, what wouldn't be? I passed on the mushy canned peas, but Howard and Robert dug in. Those two will eat anything.

Wednesday was Grandpa's Elks Club night. He was running for the office of Grand Exalted Ruler and had to be at the meeting early to work on his campaign speech. Wonder if that's anything like being the Big Poobah from *The Flintstones* movie? I could just picture him wearing Fred Flintstone's woolly mammoth hat.

After the dishes were taken care of, Grandma encouraged me to get my homework done right away so I could watch *Tony Orlando and Dawn* at eight o'clock. I'd never heard of the show, but she seemed excited about it, so I diligently worked on my various assignments. *Man, these kids have a lot of homework.* Guess they had nothing better to do anyway.

A minute before eight, I made my way down the stairs to the den. Grandma was parked in Grandpa's recliner, and Howard and Robert had the couch. Glider rocker for me again.

Tony Orlando was a Latino guy, probably in his thirties, and Dawn referred to his two African American female background singers. The first song they sang was "Knock Three Times."

"Ally, that was one of the songs they sang when we saw them live, remember?"

Nope. Wasn't me.

"Yah," I lied, trying to sound enthusiastic. I tried to picture Mom and Grandma rocking out at a concert together. Wasn't happening.

The variety show had skits, songs and guest stars, none of whom I knew. My attention drifting, I studied the interaction between Grandma and the guys as they watched. Despite the fact that the boys were teenagers, the three of them seemed to get along pretty well. At least when Howard and Robert weren't squabbling.

The show ended with the song "Tie a Yellow Ribbon Round the Old Oak Tree." *Must be a family favorite.* Grandma, Howard and Robert all sang along. It was surreal watching everyone in what was probably an ordinary moment in their lives.

As interesting as that was, I chose to pass watching another hour of TV with the group to check out Mom's classic *Nancy Drew* books in her closet. After saying goodnight, I hummed the yellow ribbon song all the way up to my room.

Got to experience a slice of Mom's life, both the good and the bad. *This has to be my last day here, right?*

Chapter 20

The light shining through the window illuminated the bright, sunny paint on my bedroom walls. *What is it going to take to get off this dumb merry-go-round?*

I was ready to get back to my seventh-grade life, and I'm sure Mom wanted to live hers as well. Unless that Richard thing had been ongoing since sixth grade. If that were the case, maybe she was happy to escape her life for a while.

Thursday's schedule was the same as Tuesday's. No interaction with Richard, but he threw me shade whenever I happened to glance his way. When it came time to walk to the high school, I hung back to make sure there were plenty of people between him and me. He was creeping me out big time.

That did the trick. We got to the high school with no incidents and jumped right into the breakfast foods unit. Mrs. Palacek was going to teach us how to broil grapefruit. *If that's not a life skill, I don't know what is.* She had us gather in groups of four by each oven, explained how to use it and went over the safety rules. Basically, how not to set ourselves or any other objects on fire.

Jane asked me to work with her, Sharon and Angela. The four of us did a stellar job of dumping a scoop of brown sugar onto four grapefruit halves. The maraschino cherry topped off our creations nicely. Oddly enough, the final product didn't taste as bad as it sounded.

After school, when Vicky and I walked home, I wanted to bring up the topic of Richard. Why was he picking on Mom? Was there some backstory? Of course, if Vicky knew it, that meant Mom knew it, so it'd probably look suspicious if I asked, so I didn't mention it.

The boys were at play practice, so I got to see the whole episode of *The Brady Bunch* without getting any crap from them. Grandpa had bowling at six-thirty, so we had a quick dinner.

After Grandpa exited the house, Grandma came down from her bedroom. She wore shorts and a t-shirt, a different look for her. At least, different than anything I'd ever seen her wear.

"Ready for volleyball?"

My eyes widened. *Mom played volleyball in seventh grade? How did I not know that?*

"Sure," I said enthusiastically. "I'll go change."

"No need to."

What? Jeans and a buttoned-down shirt were not viable volleyball gear. "That's okay. I'll be super quick." I bolted up the stairs without waiting for a reply. For the first time in four days, there was something that I'd get to enjoy doing.

The Impala was idling in the driveway when I walked out the back door. Grandma sat on the bench seat next to Grandpa. I opened the back door and slid into the car. Instinctively, I reached over my shoulder for the seat belt.

Nothing. There were no seatbelts anywhere in the car, as far as I could tell. I clung to the door arm for dear life as we took off towards St. Joseph's.

Passing the school, we continued on another two blocks and pulled into the parking lot of an old brick building directly across from the high school. Normal School was etched in stone above the doorway.

"You have a ride home, right?" Grandpa asked Grandma.

"Sally said she'd bring us back after the game."

"Have fun."

"I will," said Grandma and I in unison. We turned, exchanged glances and shrugged.

A group of women in their twenties and thirties were setting volleyballs back and forth and practicing underhand serving. There wasn't anyone my age on the court.

"I'm surprised you didn't bring your Nancy Drew book," said Grandma.

"Why would I?" I asked. Then it hit me. *This wasn't my volleyball game. It was Grandma's. Dang it.*

"Wanna shag balls before we start?"

"Nah," I said dejectedly. "I'll just watch."

Without rally scoring, the games seemed to go on forever. Grandma's team lost the match, but they did have one victory thanks to Grandma's wicked underhand serve. She had a six-point serving streak.

When we got home, Grandma started warming the TV. She mentioned that *The Waltons* came on at eight o'clock. Three TV stations. That's it. How much television can one family watch in a week?

Not that I had a problem with it. Minutes into the show, I was sucked in. The Waltons were such a nice family. Everybody liked each other.

After the show, I couldn't help myself. In the upstairs hallway, I called out to the boys, "Good night, John Boy." "Good night, Jim Bob." Not one, "Good night, Mary Ellen," or "Good night, Elizabeth." *Lame!* If those two don't get with the program, they're going to lose their '70s cred with me really quickly.

Chapter 21

Surprise, surprise, I woke up in Mom's body again. At least it was Friday. Maybe I was only sentenced to one school week in her life, and I could go back to my own life this weekend. The thought cheered me up immensely.

It was Mass day at St. Joseph's. Sounded like it was an every-week back then instead of once-a-month thing. One by one, the seventh-graders filed into the wooden pews with the padded kneelers about halfway back in the church.

Before Mass started, Father Laroche stepped in from the vestibule, a young priest on his heels. "Let's all welcome our new associate pastor, Father Dominic Jansen."

The church erupted in applause.

Holy cow! This guy is the spitting image of John Denver. He had blond hair with bangs and even round wire-rimmed glasses. *Wonder if he can sing like him?*

"Thank you for that friendly welcome!" the new priest said. "Since I'm going to be serving here for at least a year, we can be on a first-name basis. Father Dom works for me." Smiles lit the faces of the kids sitting around me. *Is this something new for them?*

From there, he went right into Mass. For his homily, Father Dom told a story about when he was in junior high school. Decent enough, kept me awake.

Turned out that this priest was a musician. For the offertory song, he played "They Will Know We are Christians" on his guitar, and he sang the, "Our Father" too.

Class times were shortened to accommodate Mass. That suited us fine. Everyone was abuzz because tonight was the first home high school football game for the season.

The minute the final bell rang, kids flung themselves out the double doors to hurry home to get ready for the game. Even Howard and Robert were going with their friends. It must be the hottest ticket in town.

The plan was for me to be at Vicky's house by six o'clock.

Mrs. Holtz was pulling weeds from her flowerbeds as I walked up. She told me to just go inside.

When I stepped into the kitchen, I saw Tammy sitting at the table. I wasn't sure what to make of her. Mom and Vicky were best friends when they were kids. Living as close to Vicky as she did, would Tammy drive a wedge between her and Mom?

Since Vicky was nowhere to be found, I felt obligated to engage in small talk. "How do you like it here?"

"So far, so good," Tammy replied.

"I heard you have a little sister."

"Unfortunately. She's always getting into my stuff and trying to hang out with me and my friends. Well, me and my old friends. I haven't really hung out with anyone here yet."

Ouch. Maybe I should make more of an effort to be nice to her. Vicky and Mom would always be friends. Maybe not best friends, but friends nonetheless. Would it hurt to have one more person for them to do stuff with for a while?

"Two brothers. Older," I added.

"Lucky."

Easy for her to say. She hadn't met Howard and Robert. I rolled my eyes.

The conversation dwindled. Just in time, Vicky appeared in her bedroom doorway. With her ready to go, the three of us filed out the back door, saying goodbye to Mrs. Holtz and Vicky's siblings as we left.

After walking three blocks, we made a pitstop at the grocery store or "supermarket" as Tammy called it. I'd asked Grandma for fifty cents before I'd left the house. After spending ten cents for a full-sized Kit Kat — score — I had enough money left for the twenty-five-cents admission to the game and a snack at halftime. That deal would be hard to beat.

With fifteen minutes until kickoff, we picked up our pace. The football field was situated on the outskirts of town, so we still had eight blocks to walk. We arrived at the admission gate just as the team captains were shaking hands in the middle of the field.

We each paid our quarter and found seats in the youth section at the end of the bleachers. Other girls from our class had spots saved, so we scurried up the concrete steps and positioned ourselves near them.

The band broke out into "The National Anthem,"

followed immediately by the school fight song. It was so strange. Closing my eyes, the sound was like any other Friday night football game I'd been to.

Once I opened my eyes again, everything looked similar to how it'd been at the last game I attended. The only difference was the people. I barely knew the girls sitting near me, and the rest of the fans were complete strangers.

With our team up seventeen to zero by the second quarter, Tammy, Vicky, Connie, Gina and I left the bleachers and ran to the open grass field. Some kids were playing *Television Tag*. Running through the list of TV shows I knew, I joined in. If I got tagged, I'd have to shout out the name of a show no one else had said, or I'd be "it."

At halftime, we went to the concession stand. Boston Baked Beans? Those things cost like three bucks at the movie theater. They were only ten cents a box here. There were some advantages to living in the '70s.

Candy in hand, we resumed our seats. The game was getting boring, so I focused on the cheerleaders and the pep band. After the final buzzer, fans ran onto the field to celebrate the blowout. Vicky, Tammy and I skirted the crowd and headed for home.

I walked in the door just as the mantle clock chimed nine times. It was still early for a weekend night, so I went upstairs, did my nightly routine, read for a while, and then went back downstairs just as the local news was concluding.

Howard lounged in the recliner. The *CBS Late Movie* came on. He thought it was interesting. That made one of us. After twenty minutes, I returned to my room. In bed, I stared at the ceiling and thought about the past five days living Mom's life. It was interesting seeing how things were back then, but they weren't necessarily the good ol' days by any means.

I had no idea how Mom put up with Richard as a classmate. If the whole school year were going to go like the first week, it would be a long one. Thank goodness it was her life and not mine. Not sure that I could handle that much stress.

Chapter 22

Apparently, I was going to have to learn. The sound of ticking came to my ears. “No,” I said out loud, covering my head with a pillow.

Facing reality, I threw the pillow to the floor and turned to face the clock. *Ten o’clock? Holy cow.* This dumb week had worn me out.

Looks like I get to see how Baby Boomers spent their weekends when they were kids. As I stretched, my stomach rumbled. First things first. Food. I sped through my morning ritual and walked downstairs. As per usual, Grandma had her spot staked out by the dining room table. She perused a page in a three-ring binder as I walked up.

“Good morning, um, Mom,” I said, getting my head back in the game.

“Good morning, Ally,” she replied.

I made my way around the table and into the kitchen. Opening the cabinet door, I noticed new cereal options. Grandma must have gone grocery shopping yesterday. Franken Berry, Apple Jacks and Raisin Bran. *Apple Jacks, it is.*

After eating, I headed out to the garage to see if there was something interesting to do. The car was gone. Grandpa must be out and about somewhere. Grabbing a wooden tennis racket and a can of white tennis balls, I shut the overhead garage door and proceeded to lob tennis balls against it.

Chasing balls ricocheting off the stone driveway and the wood-planked garage door was a workout. After a half-hour, I switched to basketball and worked on my free throws using the hoop with a rusted metal net.

Getting bored with that, I meandered to the back of the garage to see if there was a swing on the next-door neighbor's oak tree. It wasn't a spider web tree swing, but the old tire swing would do the trick. Throwing my leg over the top, I hoisted myself up. The rope scratched my skin, but it didn't bother me. It was nice to do something so normal. As I spun around, it almost seemed like I was in my real life again.

After a while, Grandma called me in for lunch. The boys weren't around. Maybe they hadn't gotten up yet.

Grandma had started her sandwich already, so I said the *Bless Us Oh Lord* prayer to myself and then bit into mine. I swallowed and then lifted up the piece of Wonder Bread to see what was inside.

"I made you your favorite today," said Grandma when she noticed me inspecting the sandwich. "Does it taste okay?"

About as good as a bologna and margarine sandwich could taste.

"It's fine," I managed to sputter after washing everything down with a swig of whole milk. I glanced at the sandwich Grandma was eating. Olive loaf? The sight was enough to gag me. Made my sandwich look great in comparison.

After lunch, I went to my room. I grabbed the first

book in Mom's Nancy Drew series, *The Secret of the Old Clock,* and started reading. Half-way through, I heard the phone ring. Grandma yelled up from the bottom of the staircase that the call was for me. After marking my place with a Snoopy bookmark, I ran downstairs to answer the phone.

"Hello," I said hesitantly.

"Hi, Allison!" I was pretty sure it was Gina.

"Hey."

"My mom said I can have a sleepover tonight. Can you come over?"

"Um, let me check with my, um, mom. Can you hold on a second?"

"Sure."

I walked from the entryway to the dining room. "Mom," I said in a whisper, holding my hand over the receiver, "Can I sleep over at Gina's tonight?"

"Sure. But, why are you whispering?"

"Just in case you said no," I replied.

"Have I ever said no before?"

How would I know? I shrugged my shoulders.

Grandma shook her head.

Maybe she always said yes to sleepovers, but it would've been fine if she'd said no today. Spending that much time with someone that I barely knew could be awkward. Besides that, I didn't even know where Gina lived. Guess now is when that City Directory will come in handy.

Heaving a sigh, I stepped back to the phone bench.

"Mom says I can come. What time do you want me there?"

Chapter 23

After all these years, Mom and Gina were still friends. Gina had been the maid of honor in Mom and Dad's wedding, and she was Brock's godmother. But the Mrs. Baker that I knew was way different than her younger self. Somewhere along the line, she'd obviously built up her self-esteem.

Hopefully, Gina would be more talkative at her house than she was at school. If not, it'd be a long night.

Mom's little flowered-cloth suitcase packed, I pedaled off on the banana bike, balancing the suitcase between the handlebars. It felt strange riding a bike without a helmet. How did Mom's generation survive to adulthood?

Fifteen minutes later, I pulled onto the grass next to the Kovac's driveway. A somewhat younger, and alive, version of the late Mrs. Kovac answered the front door when I rang the bell.

"Perfect timing. We're just getting ready to leave for Mass."

Forcing my jaw shut, I stuttered, "O—Okay."

Mrs. Kovac probably wondered why I looked like I'd seen a ghost. I'll tell you why. *Because I have!*

My feet were rooted to the ground.

Mrs. Kovac snapped me back to reality. "You can leave your bike there."

"Are you sure?" I stammered.

"No one will take it."

They're a trusting bunch. As dopey as the bike was, I'd feel bad for Mom if someone swiped it.

We walked into the living room just as Gina, and people that I assumed were her siblings, raced down the stairs and made a beeline for the kitchen. From there, they flew out the backdoor into the one-car attached garage.

The younger boy took a seat next to Gina's dad, who was behind the wheel. Mrs. Kovac slid in next to him. The older girl went into the back seat, followed by the older boy. Then Gina and I crammed in.

After church, we went back to the Kovac's for dinner. Gina's dad grilled hamburgers on their back patio while her mom sliced potatoes for French fries. Between the boys diving for food, each of us girls did manage to get a burger and a handful of fries.

When dinner was over, Gina suggested that we go explore their attic. It was filled to the gills with toys, clothes, furniture and boxes of who knew what. The vintage toys probably wouldn't pass modern safety regulations, but they were interesting to look at.

We found a box filled with letters, including one written by Mom when she was in first grade thanking Mr. Kovac for showing her class the fire station. Tired of digging through the attic, we went to the basement, and Gina got out a homemade *Michigan Rummy* board.

The boys wanted to play too. The older brother Jerry explained the rules for little Danny, since it was his first time playing. Mine too, so I listened in as well. He then divided the poker chips to start the game. As we played, the smell of chocolate wafted down the basement stairs.

A while later, Mrs. Kovac called us up for a snack. The made-from-scratch chocolate cupcakes, fresh out of the oven, melted in my mouth.

Jerry won the game. Whether it was luck or cheating was hard to tell. It never seemed like he put enough chips on the spots at the beginning of each round. Either way, it was fun. As I suspected, Gina was more animated with her family than she was around her classmates, so I enjoyed her company.

We went upstairs at nine o'clock, and instead of talking or listening to the radio, after we had our nightgowns on and got into bed, Gina turned off the light and said goodnight.

The bed was comfortable enough, but it was so early that it took forever to fall asleep. Her clock had little metal plates that flipped every time a minute passed. I swore I heard those dumb plates flip a hundred times before I finally zonked out.

A moment later, or so it seemed, a hand shook my shoulder. Opening my eyes, I spotted Gina.

"What time is it?" I croaked out.

"Six-forty-five."

"Why are you waking me up?"

"I've been up for an hour already. I was getting bored. Besides, it's time for breakfast."

The smell of pancakes floated past my nostrils. That was all it took to get me fully awake. I scampered behind Gina as she went down to the first floor.

Bacon sizzled in a cast-iron skillet on the back burner of the stove. Now I was really getting hungry. The boys came barreling down the steps a minute after us, their hair sticking up like Alfalfa's in *The Little Rascals* movie.

Breakfast tasted just as good as it smelled. After thanking Gina's parents for letting me sleep over, I grabbed the flowered suitcase and hopped on Mom's bike to head home. It wasn't even eight o'clock. Hopefully, someone would be up to let me in.

Chapter 24

The garage stall was empty. Grandpa must have gone somewhere. After I put Mom's bike away, I went inside to unpack her suitcase. By the time I got back downstairs, Grandpa was pulling into the driveway.

He walked in the back door carrying a newspaper and two boxes of Mrs. Karl's cake donuts. One box held glazed donuts with chopped peanuts and the other one frosted chocolate. Even though I'd just finished breakfast at Gina's, this treat was impossible to resist. The waxy chocolate frosting from the donut clung to the roof of my mouth. It took a whole cup of milk to wash that thing down.

Grandpa drank his coffee while he perused the paper. He was engrossed in a story on the front page, so I checked out the headlines on the back.

"Want to read the funnies?"

Funnies? "I guess."

He handed me a section of the paper. "Here you go."

"Thanks." I paged through the paper. When I came to a whole page of comics, it dawned on me what he was talking about.

While most of the comic strips were unfamiliar to me, I did recognize a couple.

By eight forty-five, everybody was downstairs, the boys dressed for church like Grandpa. Grandma wore her nightgown, bathrobe and slippers. She poured herself a cup of coffee and shuffled off to the dining room. The sound of the Bic lighter flicking came to my ears. First cigarette of the day. *How she's dodged the lung cancer bullet all these years is beyond me.*

The guys headed off to church. After the car pulled away, Grandma went upstairs to take a bath and wash and set her hair. With the downstairs to myself and not much else to do, I went into the bathroom and scaled the wall of cabinets.

Mom shopped year-round for Christmas gifts and hid them in the upper cabinets. Maybe Grandma did too. Since I planned to be out of here by then, there'd be no harm checking to see what Mom, Howard and Robert would be getting for Christmas.

Sure enough, I saw a bag in the back corner of the closet. Balancing on the middle shelf, I inched towards it until I could grab it with my right hand. Peeking inside, I saw a Texas Instruments box. A calculator? That couldn't possibly be a Christmas gift.

So much for that. Wasn't even worth the climb. A full-fledged yawn broke out of me. My time would be better spent taking a nap. I trudged to the formal living room, grabbed the afghan Grandma had crocheted and laid on the couch.

Pulling the afghan under my chin, I realized that it was one we still had at home. The thought comforted me, and I was asleep within seconds.

Before I knew it, Grandpa and the boys were back from church. I wanted to snooze a little longer, but Howard and Robert were rambunctious and getting louder by the minute.

Hair wound in prickly rollers with pink sticks securing them to her head, Grandma stomped downstairs, pointed at the boys wrestling in the den, and shouted. "Out!"

Howard stopped mid-pin. "We're just goofing around."

"You can goof around outside where you won't break anything. Go!"

With one last twist of Robert's arm, Howard dropped him to the ground. He left the house with Robert one step behind him. The look in his eyes made me think he'd be seeking revenge once he was out of Grandma's sight.

The sound of the refrigerator opening let me know that Grandma was starting lunch. I didn't want to get roped into helping, so I grabbed my sandals from the back closet and headed out after the guys.

Surprisingly enough, they weren't killing each other when I got to the back yard. They'd actually grabbed a football from the garage and were playing catch.

"Can I play too?" I asked.

"I don't care," said Howard. I took that as a yes and went to the far side of the yard. For a bit, the three of us threw the ball clockwise around the triangle that we formed, covering most of the backyard.

Then Howard suggested we run some plays. We took turns playing center, wide receiver and quarterback. When it was my turn to be quarterback, I took one snap from Howard and one from Robert, with both complaining that I couldn't throw far enough. I switched to wide receiver, with Robert as center.

"Hut," said Howard, motioning me to go deep. I ran a little bit.

"Further."

I ran a few more feet.

"Further." I ran to the edge of the yard. He threw the football, and I made the catch. With a sense of victory, I streaked toward the sidewalk, the official goal line.

Before I knew what was happening, my feet slid out from under me, and I skidded on my rear end the last foot of the sidewalk, coming to a halt at the grass line.

Pain immediately tore through my legs. I couldn't help myself and started bawling. Specks of blood from my scraped-up thighs dotted the sidewalk. The boys ran over, each grabbing me under one armpit, and helped me hobble back to the house. Whey they got me up the stoop and into the backdoor, Grandma rushed over to me.

"What did you boys do to her?" Grandma asked, assessing my injuries.

"Nothing," they said in unison. "We were just playing football, and she ran for a deep pass and slid on the sidewalk," said Robert.

Grandma glanced between the boys with a skeptical look.

"Back outside, you two," she yelled. She put her arm around my shoulders and helped me over to the kitchen sink. Letting the water run for a bit, she grabbed a clean dishrag, wet it, wrung it out and applied it to the deepest cut.

Holy crap, that hurt! I started crying again, but that didn't deter Grandma. She rinsed out the dishrag and started working on the smaller areas. As the pain diminished, my tears finally did too.

With the blood washed off, Grandma went into the bathroom. I heard the medicine cabinet opening. She came back with a small brown bottle.

"What's that?" I asked suspiciously.

"Mecuricome."

"Mecuricome? What are you going to do with it?"

"Put in on the cuts." She looked at me, her hazel eyes showing concern. "Did you bump your head too?"

"No."

She felt the back of my head just to be sure, then dropped to her knees so she could apply the gold-colored liquid to my scrapes.

"This might sting a little," she said.

That was an understatement. I gritted my teeth so I wouldn't blurt out what was at the tip of my tongue. *Are you freaking kidding me? It hurts like a...* My eyes stung with tears.

"It'll help you heal faster."

Likely story. If that stuff was so good, why hadn't I heard of it before?

The torture complete, I dragged my miserable body out of the kitchen, slowly making my way to the stairs. I ascended the staircase, gingerly lifting one foot after the other. At the top of the landing, I shuffled to my room and eased myself onto my bed, face down.

I hate this stupid life! When is this torture going to be over?

A while later, Grandma came up and asked if I wanted to have lunch. My appetite was gone, so I declined. I sniffled into the bedspread, feeling sorry for myself and for Mom. Six whole days and I'd already wrecked her body. Hopefully, this wouldn't leave any scars.

Chapter 25

I spent the rest of the afternoon on my stomach listening to the radio. By dinnertime, my legs felt somewhat better, so I crept downstairs. Looking out the dining room window, I saw Grandpa dumping charcoal into the grill on the back patio.

When I got to the kitchen, Grandma was putting the finishing touch — sliced boiled eggs — onto a bowl of potato salad. A Jell-O salad sat on the counter to her right.

"Feeling better?" she asked.

"A little bit. It still stings."

She nodded and went back to slicing eggs with the paring knife. I scooted around her and opened the fridge. A plate of raw chicken pieces and a bowl of barbeque sauce sat on the middle shelf. Barbequed chicken? My mouth began to water.

Out of curiosity, I shuffled to the back door and went down the steps of the stoop to watch Grandpa man the charcoal grill. Robert was perched on the top wall of the porch. All the windows were open and instrumental music coming from the jumbo record player in the dining room could be heard from where we were. Grandpa hummed along to the catchy tune.

"What's this song called… Dad?" The dad word still felt unnatural.

Robert rolled his eyes.

"Don't you recognize it?" Grandpa asked, looking up at me.

I shrugged my shoulders.

"'A Taste of Honey.' Herb Alpert and the Tijuana Brass."

"Oh, yeah, that's right."

I watched as he squirted lighter fluid over the charcoal. Even though my legs were tired, I remained standing. Settling down on the scratchy stone surface of the stoop would be painful. Besides that, Robert took up the whole top spot, and the next ledge held Grandpa's grilling supplies and a can of Pabst Blue Ribbon beer.

The lighter fluid can empty, Grandpa turned and walked to the garage. Once he was out of sight, Robert grabbed the can of beer and took a swig. *Are you kidding me?*

Words spilled out of my mouth before I could stop them. "Robby, what the heck are you doing?"

"Just getting a drink. What's it to you?" he shot back.

"If Dad sees you, he'll kill you."

"Well, he didn't, so now what? Gonna tattle on me?"

I hated it when Brock and Brayden ratted on me, so I had no intention of doing that to Robert. But I seriously couldn't believe what I just saw. *Was this when it all started?* I wondered, thinking of the man I knew who'd struggled with alcohol and drug addiction most of his life. *Should I be doing an intervention?*

It was a dilemma. If I was only here for a short time, I didn't think it would be a wise idea to alter anyone's future, good or bad. I decided to let it drop.

Grandpa came back a few seconds later with a new can of lighter fluid, finished wetting the charcoal, then lit a match and flicked it onto the charcoal to start the fire. Once the coals turned gray, he went into the house for the meat.

Throwing caution to the wind, I blurted out, "Don't even think about taking another drink, Robby."

Robert stuck his tongue out at me.

Plate of chicken in one hand, the small bowl of barbeque sauce in the other, Grandpa came back outside and, after setting the bowl down, proceeded to stab each piece of chicken and place it onto the round grate that covered the shallow grill. It took quite a while for the chicken to cook. When the chicken skin had black lines seared into it, Grandpa smothered each piece with sauce, first on the top side, then flipped them over and brushed the flat side.

After a tasty dinner, everyone took off separate ways. The boys had homework they'd procrastinated doing all weekend. Injured or not, I still had to help with dishes. Grudgingly, I picked up the flour sack dishtowel. Grandpa stepped into the den to warm up the TV. The sound of a clock ticking came to my ears. *60 Minutes? That show's been on forever. Grandpa still watches it.*

At seven o'clock, the boys raced back downstairs to watch *The Wonderful World of Disney.* Tonight's feature was *Bedknobs and Broomsticks.* Even though the movie was made for younger kids, Howard and Robert seemed to dig it. With the concluding notes playing, Howard turned off the TV, and everyone retreated to their rooms.

In bed, I repeated the prayer I'd said every night this week. "Please, God, let me have my life back." Hearing nothing, I heaved a sigh and rolled over.

Chapter 26

"Monday, Monday. Can't trust that day." No truer words had ever been spoken, or sung, for that matter. Getting ready for the day, I listened to the entire song, still in disbelief that what I hoped would be a one-week sentence had been extended.

Obviously, God was doing this to me, but why? Was my real life going on now without me? Did He have some cosmic lesson I had to learn before He'd let me go back?

Week number two, here I go. A sigh escaped my lips.

Big, gray clouds stretched across the sky when I stepped out the back door. "Please, don't rain," I said out loud. Mom's hooded sweatshirt would only last so long before the water soaked through to my clothes.

Charles and Sherry, wearing oversized shirts to keep their school clothes clean, were finishing their breakfast when I got to Vicky's. Crissy pranced out from her bedroom when she heard my voice.

She threw herself into my arms. I picked her up and gently gave her a hug. Crissy chatted away as I set her back down. Her voice reminded me of Alvin and the other Chipmunks.

With breakfast done, Charles and Sherry brushed their teeth and headed out the door, seven-forty on the dot. That was, according to Mom's watch, not the

Holtz's clock. I bided my time waiting for Vicky by making small talk with Mrs. Holtz as she wiped down the kitchen table.

She didn't seem to be overly friendly, so the conversation was stilted. I was more than happy when Vicky raced into the kitchen, plastic schoolbag clutched in her hand. On the way to school, Vicky filled me in about their weekend at her aunt and uncle's.

We got to school before the bell rang and got out our Literature books. The books I had read over the weekend earned Mom two stickers for her apple.

I was leery when it came time for Music because of what Richard had done to me last week. Thankfully the sopranos were on the opposite side of the room from Richard and the other bass, Ronald Meyer. We worked on a song called "Joshua Fought the Battle of Jericho," or "Joshua fit the Battle of Jericho," as Sister insisted it be sung.

Thanks for the earworm, Sister. It was going to take forever to get that dumb song out of my head.

Since I was off lunch duty this week, I ate with the girls from Mom's class and went out to play soccer right after lunch. A group of first-grade girls tagged us after as we crossed the playground. They begged us to push them on the merry-go-round.

Not being into little kids — even my own brothers — I would've kept walking, but one of those twerps happened to be Jane's neighbor, so she said she'd do it. She asked if I'd hang back and help push. As much as I wanted to get to the soccer field before teams were picked, I said I would. Again, the thought, "What would Mom do?" nagged me.

With the merry-go-round spinning at top speed and all the swings flying after the under-ducks that Jane and I provided, we took off for the soccer field. By the time we got there, the game had started, so we each went on a different side.

There were no pinnies for the goalies, so the furthest person back on the field played goalie and could use their hands. More than one argument broke out on the field as it wasn't always easy to determine who was the furthest back, and consequently, multiple people were picking up the ball. Brenda's ankle was still wrapped, so she acted as the informal referee from the top of the climbing tower.

After recess, we worked on story problems in Math the whole hour. When the bell rang, Sister Joachim walked into the room, carrying a cardboard box lined with a half dozen microscopes. She told us to go outside and gather organic material to analyze.

Scurrying out the front door, we gathered twigs and leaves and even chalk dust. After we'd checked out the magnified images, Sister instructed us to scrape some skin cells from our arms and brush them onto the glass plates to see what they looked like magnified.

I glanced over at Vicky to gauge her reaction. She had a crusty rash on her forearms. Wonder how that'd look under the microscope? As much as I'd like to find out, there was no nice way to ask, and I didn't want to risk getting her mad again.

Dutifully, I scratched the back of my hand and

brushed skin onto the glass plate. Closing my right eye, I peered into the eyepiece with my left eye.

"Dog skin look any different than human skin?" asked Richard in a low voice.

My head shot up. He was planted not a foot away from me. Narrowing my eyes at him, I returned to my position over the microscope, even though I'd lost interest in the project. When I heard him step back to his microscope, I walked to my desk, sat down and stared at the chalkboard.

Those dorky glasses actually came in handy for once. They hid the tears clinging to my lower lashes. *I cannot stand that guy! Why does he keep picking on me?*

After what felt like an eternity, the bell finally rang. We had five minutes between classes. I rushed to the girls' bathroom, found an empty stall, locked the door and grabbed a chunk of toilet paper to wipe my eyes. I flushed it afterwards, so the other girls there would think I'd been using the bathroom, not crying like a big baby.

Chapter 27

Sister Cecilia breezed back into the classroom. I perked up a bit when she said we'd be discussing U.S. involvement in the Vietnam War from a Catholic perspective. Not that I was interested in a war that had ended close to forty years before I was born, but a class discussion might mean no homework tonight, and I was all for that.

Some kids spoke in favor of the war, saying it was stopping communism from taking over the world. Others said the U.S. shouldn't have to babysit the entire planet. I had no opinion either way, but even if I had, I wouldn't have voiced my thoughts. Not worth putting myself in Richard's crosshairs again. Once was enough for one day.

Gym class was decent because Mr. Kovac had the boys and girls on opposite ends of the grass field playing kickball. With no chance of running into Richard, I could enjoy the game.

After I returned home from school, the smell of baked goods came to me before I even reached the stoop. Through the screen door, I saw homemade pretzels cooling on the kitchen table.

These were even better than the pretzels from the mall. They were warm and chewy, and the chunky salt was the perfect topping.

Pretzel in hand, I wandered over to the stove and peeked under the lid of a pot that had something boiling in it. Steam rolled out and fogged my glasses.

Boiled meat? That's a new one. I put the cover back on and checked out the pot on the back burner. Cubed potatoes. Pistachio pudding cooled in glass parfait dishes in the fridge. School was crappy, but at least dinner would be good.

Good was an understatement. Corned beef was delicious. *Why doesn't Mom ever make this?*

The evening ended in what was probably a typical fashion for Mom back then. Homework, reading, TV. No Yankees game, though. I settled in and to watch a rerun of *Gunsmoke* with Grandpa.

Howard was at play practice, so I shared the couch with Robert. We each had our own cushion, but he kept creeping his foot onto mine just to be annoying. Each time he did it, I ground my teeth and yelled, "Stop it."

After the fourth time, Grandpa lost his patience. "Upstairs, Robert."

With Grandpa's attention back to the TV, I made a snotty face at Robert as he left the den. Two could play that game.

Chapter 28

By the time Tuesday rolled around, the gloomy gray clouds had passed, and sunlight flooded through the kitchen windows.

"Don't forget your jacket," Grandma yelled from upstairs when she heard me open the back door.

"It's nice out, don't need one," I shouted back.

"Is the temperature above sixty?"

I glanced at the thermometer outside the kitchen window. *By the time Grandma comes downstairs, it will be.*

"It's all good," I said vaguely. "See you after school."

When Vicky and I got to school twenty minutes later, Angela Bergner met us on the sidewalk in front of the building.

"Hey," she said, handing small envelopes to me and Vicky. "I'm having a birthday party a week from Saturday. It'd be cool if you can come."

I grabbed the envelope and pulled out a flat invitation, neatly written out in mom-type handwriting. Glancing at the details, I looked up at Angela and nodded. "That works for me." *Mom's social calendar can't be that full.*

"Cool. By the way, my mom only let me invite six girls from our class, so don't mention this to anyone other than Connie, Patty, Jane and Tammy."

"We'll keep it on the down-low," I said. Angela looked at me a bit oddly. "I mean, we'll be cool about it and not say anything to the other girls."

When Angela turned to hand an invitation to Jane, Vicky and I walked into school, and she immediately broke into a huge grin, her silver braces glinting in the sunlight.

"This is going to be great! Mrs. Bergner's a real-life Mrs. Brady. She'll have every detail planned out ahead of time, so the party will be so cool." Vicky clapped her hands together. "You've seen the monthly menus she posts on their fridge, right?"

Since she assumed that I had, I went along with it. "Yah, for sure. She's super organized."

With Jane and Angela one step behind us, we got to our room, and the four of us circled up with Connie, Patty and Tammy, chattering in hushed tones about the party until the bell rang.

After the mad dash for our desks, I leaned over in my seat and whispered to Vicky. "Are you surprised Tammy was invited? Angela doesn't even know her."

"She can't stand anyone from the popular group, so that eliminated all those girls from the running. I'm not sure how she chose from the rest of us. Just glad I made the cut."

"Me too," I replied. *At least I think I am.* It was weird planning for anything when each day in Groovyville could — if there is a God — be my last one. This time-travel thing has to end at some point.

On the bottom of the invitation, it said to bring records. Mom only had a few 45s in the box in her closet. Maybe Uncle Howard would be a decent human being for once and let me borrow some of his.

Between classes, Patty approached me and Vicky. "Peggy and I got *Twister* for Christmas. I'm going to see if I can sneak it out of the house without her seeing. She'd have a conniption if she found out."

I had no idea what a conniption was, or who Peggy was for that matter, but I knew what *Twister* was because my friends and I loved that game. "Cool!" I said with enthusiasm.

Connie joined us and said she planned to bring her sister's hot rollers so we could do each other's hair. That'd be interesting considering what little hair I had on my head, thanks to Mom's brilliant idea to get the shag cut. Tammy turned from her seat and whispered, "I can bring a couple of bottles of my older sister's nail polish."

Throughout the morning, my mind wandered to the upcoming party. Assuming I'd still be around, I hoped Vicky and I could go in on a gift together. I had no idea what Angela was into.

After lunch, a group of us seventh-graders walked toward the soccer field. A little girl jumping rope sang, "Cinderella, dressed in yella, went downtown to see her fella, on her way, her girdle busted, how many people were disgusted?" That classic had survived through the years.

Soccer captains were being picked when we stepped onto the field. "Eeny, meenie, miny, mo." McKenzie McFadden and Bobbi Jo Howell won, so it looked like it'd be the popular girls against the not-popular girls today. *Bring it on!*

In Science, Richard caught my attention as he slouched in his desk, folding a piece of notebook paper into a small triangle. Teeing it up, he flicked the paper through the goal that Andrew Wickert made with his fingers. After his third score, he turned towards me.

"Ruff, ruff," came from his lips as he pretended to cough. I spun my head back to the front of the room. *That guy is freakin' annoying.*

Next hour, Father Dom stopped by our Religion class. He had us arrange our desks into a circle, and then he walked from kid to kid, asking each of us to say something about us that made us unique.

For a moment, I considered saying that I was a time-traveler and was just here making a pitstop in my mom's seventh-grade body, but thought better of it. I went with something lame about my dad being in the Air Force and how many places we'd lived.

After everyone had a chance to say something, Father Dom grabbed his guitar. He strummed a few notes and then sang, "I'm leaving on a jet plane..." Maybe he really *was* John Denver.

After Religion, we hustled to the high school for Home Ec. Sewing today. I pulled out the paper bag that Grandma had sent with me to school. Pink gingham fabric, matching thread, polyester stuffing, a pipe cleaner and two googly plastic eyes. Looks like I'd be making a stuffed pig. At least it wasn't a dog. Richard would be all over that.

After school, Angela caught up with me and Vicky as we approached High Avenue.

"Allison, think I can come over for supper tonight?

Liver and onions on the menu at our house."

Since Grandpa worked on Tuesday nights, Grandma could be okay with it. "Sure," I said, in a less-than-excited tone.

When we reached our house, Angela and I waved goodbye to Vicky, headed in the back door and went up to my room.

"Should we start our homework?" I suggested.

"Are you kidding?" said Angela. "I'll whip through it at home. Let's listen to the radio."

"Um, okay. Let me go downstairs quick and ask my mom if it's all right for you to eat here."

"Go for it."

Permission from Grandma granted; I followed the blasting music back up to my room.

"Wanna make some prank phone calls?" asked Angela, a conspiratorial look on her face.

Was this chick serious? "Can't," I lied, trying to come up with something on the spot.

Angela eyed me unbelievingly.

"Last time I got caught. My mom grounded me for a week. I don't want to miss your party."

"I hear ya," she acknowledged. "How bout we call WWKA and request a song."

That was a safer alternative. "That sounds good... As long as you do the calling."

After hearing "Bennie and the Jets," Angela suggested we go downstairs to watch TV. She wanted to catch *Gilligan's Island*. Holy cow, there were a lot of dumb shows back in the day. At least from my perspective. Angela thought it was hilarious.

Robert finished his paper route in time to watch the last ten minutes of the show.

"Hey, Angela," he said before flopping into Grandpa's recliner.

"Hey, Rob," she replied, batting her eyelashes.

Good grief.

The two of them laughed at Gilligan's antics as I impatiently waited for the show to end. As the final music faded away, Grandma called us to eat. Tomato soup and grilled cheese sandwiches made with soft, white bread. Angela picked the perfect day to come over.

After we said the meal prayer, Robert grabbed the bread bag and emptied it onto his plate. My eyes widened in astonishment. He pulled a Snoopy sticker from the bottom of the bag.

"Did you really have to do that, Robby?" asked Grandma. She probably would have yelled at him if Angela hadn't been there. Good timing on his part.

Since I was going to accompany Angela partway home, Grandma let me off the hook, and I got out of drying dishes. Having her over wasn't that bad after all. Robert certainly seemed to enjoy her company.

Chapter 29

Grandma was excited about a new show called *Happy Days*. I diligently finished my homework and scooted downstairs before it started.

On the way down the steps, I heard the song lyrics "rocking around the clock," coming from the TV. *Must be the theme song.* I grabbed a seat on the couch before Howard and Robert got to the den.

The show was set in the 1950s, Grandma's high-school years. It was about a group of teenagers growing up in Milwaukee. Richie Cunningham was the main kid, and his friend Fonzie was the cool guy in the show. Grandma was enamored from the opening scene.

Next in the lineup was *M*A*S*H.* It was a comedy about field surgeons working during the Korean War. The guy named Hawkeye reminded me so much of Grandpa's brother John. He was funny and snarky, just like him. That show was more my speed.

The retro version of *Hawaii 5-0* came on right after that. This was a must-see in my eyes.

"Mom, can I stay up?"

"Is your homework done?"

"I did it before *Happy Days*."

"That's fine, but you need to get your teeth brushed and put your nightgown on first."

The words were barely out of her mouth, and I was

running up the stairs. I flew back down in time to hear the theme song.

When *Hawaii 5-0* ended, I said goodnight to everyone and made my way up the stairs. Pausing on the top landing, my eyes swept over the piano. At dinner, Grandma mentioned that I'd be starting lessons again next week.

How much more torture do I have to go through in this dumb life? After begging Mom for a year, she'd finally let me quit piano lessons after fifth grade. I knew I wasn't a natural; it just took her longer to come to that same conclusion.

If I was still here next week, I'd have to figure out where Mom took lessons and who the teacher was. Even if I accomplished that, it'd be hard to explain if I was way behind Mom.

Maybe I should beg Grandma to let me quit. Mom might actually thank me in the end.

Chapter 30

With temperatures still hovering around sixty Wednesday, I slipped out of the house jacket-free.

The highlight of the school day was Gym class. Mr. Kovac met us outside, a nylon World War II parachute bunched in his arms. Laid out on the football field, it was huge, but it didn't weigh much.

He instructed us kids to each grab onto the parachute with two hands. As we lifted it above our heads, it filled with air. A couple of kids at a time were told to let go and run underneath it but get back out before it deflated. After everyone had a turn, we inflated the parachute once again, and all ran to the middle while still hanging on to the edge. Then we ran out and inflated it one more time. Everyone was huffing and puffing by the time we were done.

After school, we had Girl Scouts. The girls in Mom's troop were working on their Babysitting badge, so a nurse from the hospital came in to talk about child safety. To meet the rest of the requirements for the badge, all the girls would have to babysit real kids. I'd let Mom deal with that when she got back.

Grandma had meatloaf and baked potatoes on the table when I got home. It was the same recipe that Mom made. The ketchup and brown sugar combo on top was the best.

The premiere of *Little House on the Prairie* was

tonight. I'd seen it in reruns but wanted to watch it live, so Grandma let me skip drying the pots and pans so I could see the start. After the dishes were put away, Grandma joined me in the den. Wonder how freaked out she'd be if I predicted how the show ended?

Tony Orlando and Dawn capped off TV for the night. When it was over, I headed up to my room to finish one of Mom's *Nancy Drew* books. There'd be another dot on her reading apple tomorrow.

A gentle rain fell Thursday morning as I left for school. I put the hood up on my nylon jacket and ran all the way to Vicky's. Her dad hadn't left for work yet, so he offered to give everyone a ride to St. Joseph's. We all piled in the back of the Holtz Furniture & Flooring delivery van.

It'd be neat to ride in Mr. Holtz's convertible sometime. For the time being, it sat on four concrete blocks in their driveway.

"When's the car going to be finished, Mr. Holtz?"

"As soon as I can find the parts I need. And the time to install them," Mr. Holtz replied.

"Or when H, E, double toothpicks freezes over," Vicky whispered to me before slamming the panel door shut. "That car has been on blocks since before Crissy was born."

"Maybe he'll have it done by the time you're in high school," I offered. "You could cruise Main Avenue on Friday nights."

"Heck, yah!" said Vicky. "That'd be so cool!"

The rainy day made the day drag. We couldn't go out for recess, so after lunch, we went back to our classroom to play a game called *7-Up*. Seven kids were picked to be "it" and went up to the front of the classroom. Everyone else sat in their desks, and then Sister Cecilia chanted, "Heads down, thumbs up, time to play 7-Up."

We rested our heads on our desks, closed our eyes and put our thumbs up. The people who were "it" walked around the room and touched somebody's thumb. If your thumb was touched, you lowered it. The people who were "it" returned to the front of the room, and then Sister Cecilia said, "Heads up, Seven Up." The kids who had their thumbs touched stood up and got one guess as to who touched their thumbs. If they got it right, they went to the front of the room and took the place of the person who touched them.

I wasn't "it" to start, but I did get my thumb tapped. When I stood, I scanned the seven kids in the front and would put money on it that Richard hadn't touched me. Besides his personal vendetta against Mom, I doubted that cool boys would touch the thumbs of not-cool girls.

Looking everyone else over, I caught Richard's eye. He mouthed, "Ruff, ruff." My face grew hot, and I blurted out, "Sharon Foster."

Vicky scrunched up her face like I was nuts. I'm sure she wondered why I hadn't guessed her name. I'd figured it was her but didn't want to stand at the front of the room by Richard. The game was not fun anymore. I counted down the minutes until the bell rang.

At least I didn't have to worry about Richard when we left for Home Ec. With rain pouring down, everyone ran the three blocks to the high school as fast as we could, trying to dodge the puddles. Gina and Gary were in the back of the group, struggling to keep up with the rest of us. But it was every man for himself, so I tugged my hood around my head and ran full speed.

It was still raining when I got home from school, so Grandma suggested that I go over to Grandma Schmitt's house. I'd never met the neighborhood grandma before, since she'd died before I was born, but apparently, Mom used to hang with her after school to play *500 Rummy*. And get home-cooked snacks.

Cards and snacks sounded good to me on such a gloomy afternoon, so I crossed the street, went up the wooden steps, walked into the screened-in porch and knocked.

Opening the door, a smile crossed the old lady's wrinkled face. "Well, look who's here," said Grandma Schmitt. "Seventh grade must be keeping you busy; it's been a while since you've come by."

I gave her a quick perusal. Plump, short-waisted, white hair and wearing a dress that looked like something from the gangster days. Thick nylon pull-up socks and sensible pumps like the sisters wore — brown though instead of black — finished the look.

"Yah, um, it's been busy. We get homework almost every night."

"Oy, the students in our one-room schoolhouse used to complain about too much schoolwork too. They never had to take any home, though. Only so many books to go around, and they all had chores after school. The cows weren't going to milk themselves." Grandma Schmitt cackled.

"Take a seat, Ally; I've got some side pork cooking."

Whatever that was, it smelled delicious.

A gas stove was visible from the chair. Spattering sounded from the cast iron skillet on the front burner. Grandma Schmitt grabbed a crocheted hot pad and set the pan on a different burner. She poked a couple pieces of meat onto a fork and set them on two small plates.

One bite and I was hooked. It was like bacon, but better. The fat on the edges was crisp and curled up, and it was super salty.

After our snack, Grandma grabbed a deck of worn playing cards from the top of an old-fashioned pedal sewing machine and started shuffling. Cards dealt, she reached back over to the sewing machine and gabbed a piece of scratch paper and a nubby pencil.

It'd been a while since I'd played *500 Rummy*, but it came back to me soon enough.

"Phew! Glad I didn't get caught with Black Betty in my hand," Grandma said after the first round, tapping the queen of spades. "Would've cost me forty points."

No one said *500 Rummy* was politically correct. It was my turn to shuffle. I glanced around the house while making a bridge with the cards. The place looked like a Depression-era museum.

Eight hands in, Grandma Schmitt hit the five-hundred mark. Getting up from my seat, I assured her that I wouldn't be a stranger, then ran back home for dinner.

Volleyball again tonight. This time I brought my homework to work on between games. Grandma and I got dropped off at home just in time to catch The Waltons. With my assignments done, I got to stay up for a cop show, *The Streets of San Francisco.*

Grandpa got home from bartending at quarter to ten, so he sat down and watched the last part of the show with us. He and Grandma pointed out sites that they recognized from their trip to California for the Elks national convention last year.

It was nice hanging out, listening to them talk and reminiscing. They'd gotten divorced when Mom was in high school, so I'd never seen the two of them interact in a cordial manner. I did what I could to burn that happy memory into my brain.

Chapter 31

Clouds still covered the sky Friday morning, but at least the rain had stopped. Our class buzzed as everyone talked about their plans for the weekend. The biggest item on my agenda was a babysitting job that Grandma had lined up for me. I was less-than enthused, but at least Mom would earn her Babysitting badge.

As the other girls went out to the soccer field after lunch, I ran to the bathroom. Leaving, I noticed Richard getting a drink from the water fountain. Hoping to avoid him, I turned to go up the stairs on the opposite end of the building.

Unfortunately, he spotted me. “Where you going, dog? Someone taking you out for a walk?”

I glared at him. “You think you’re so funny.”

He sneered at me and turned back to the fountain. I scurried over to the stairway.

“Better get outside so you can bury your bone before the bell rings.”

Refusing to respond, I bounded up the stairs. Out of his sight, I leaned against the wall and blinked back tears. I wallowed in my misery for a minute until I saw Miss White approach the top of the second flight of stairs. Turning towards the double doors, I wiped my eyes with my sleeve and stepped outside.

Before heading to the soccer field, I scanned the

playground to make sure that Richard was on the football field. I didn't want to cross that moron's path again.

The rest of the afternoon, I didn't feel well. It was a huge relief when the last bell finally rang, and me and Vicky started our walk home. Even though I wanted to say something to her about Richard, I didn't. I still wasn't sure if this was an ongoing thing or if it just started when I got into town.

That night I went to the Jones' to babysit. Sergeant Jones was excited to show me his new stereo system. It had fancy speakers and woofers and things that I couldn't care less about. The demonstration was a waste of time. I had no intention of touching the thing.

After the kids ate their fish sticks and store-bought French fries, we sat around their black-and-white TV and watched *Flipper*. Then we played games until it was time for the three rugrats to go to bed.

The Joneses pulled into the gravel driveway at five minutes to eight. I gave them the report, and Sergeant Jones handed me five quarters. Fifty cents an hour for when the kids were awake and a quarter an hour when they were in bed. *Could you be a bigger cheapskate?* That being said, the kids were actually well-behaved, and it was easy to watch them.

I ran home, kicked off my shoes and tossed my coat in the direction of the back closet. After racing through the kitchen and the front entryway, I saw Howard and Robert positioned on the couch with Grandma in the recliner. *Dang!*

Since it was Friday, I was determined to stay up as late as possible. The last show of the night was *The Midnight Special.* I didn't know any of the bands, but the host was a funny guy named Wolfman Jack. That made it worth staying up.

Once I was in bed, I tried lying on my stomach, but it hurt, so I rolled onto my back and giving a sigh, shut my eyes and drifted off to sleep.

Saturday morning, I woke at nine-thirty, and after inhaling a bowl of Froot Loops, dialed Vicky. That buck and a quarter that I'd earned was burning a hole in my pocket. Maybe we could go to the movie theater.

On Saturday afternoons back then, the Grand Theater showed kid-friendly movies. This week's feature was *Herbie Rides Again*, a comedy about a talking car. The matinee started at two. If we left by one o'clock, we'd have enough time to walk downtown to get a gift for Angela before the movie began.

We made it to Woolworth's Five & Dime by one-twenty.

"Oh, perfect," said Vicky when she spotted two copies of the record "Seasons in the Sun" on the rack. "We can each get a copy!"

I debated a few seconds and then grabbed the record from Vicky's outstretched hand. "Cool," I said, feigning enthusiasm for one of the sappiest songs I'd ever heard. If Mom doesn't like this song, she'll be perplexed when she finds it in her record box.

Vicky flipped through more records. "We need to find something for Angela." She tipped each record forward with her pointer finger and looked at the titles. "She's kind of into harder rock. Can you think of anything she'd like, Allison?"

"No," I said truthfully. "Just take what looks good to you."

She pulled out three 45s and handed them to me. "Radar Love," "Smokin' In the Boys Room," "Beach Baby." They played "Beach Baby" on the radio at least once a day, so at least I recognized one of them. "Looks good to me."

"Cool. Let's pick out some lip gloss and nail polish. That should be enough."

The makeup department featured a big display of Lip Smackers. After sniffing various tubes, we agreed on the watermelon flavor. With the thought, *What would Marcia Brady do?* I searched for the brightest shade of nail polish that I could find. Cotton Candy Pink. If that doesn't say *I'm a groovy 1970s chick,* nothing would. Vicky nodded in approval.

With time on our hands, we meandered the aisle featuring Halloween merchandise.

"I can't believe they already have this stuff on display," said Vicky. "Halloween's more than a month away."

Are you kidding? I thought of telling her that in the era I come from, they start putting Halloween crap out in August but instead replied, "I know. But, it's kind of cool to look at."

"Will your mom let you get a new costume this year?" Vicky asked. "You've been wearing that witch's cape and mask since first grade."

Good question. "Doubt it," I replied, remembering

pictures of Mom in that costume multiple years. *Hopefully, I'll be out of here before Halloween.* The thought of wearing that plastic mask with the holes for eyes and the slit to breathe through gagged me.

"There's one advantage to having younger sisters," noted Vicky. I hand my costumes down to them, and I get a new one every couple years."

"Lucky!"

"Hey, I have an idea," said Vicky, after looking at a few more costumes. "Let's be bobby-soxers for Halloween."

The idea sounded great. That is, if I actually knew what a bobby-soxer was.

"We can each wear one of our mom's skirts, and maybe Bobbi Jo can draw a poodle out of felt to decorate them." Vicky put more thought into the project. "Then we can wear one of our dad's white buttoned-down shirts and finish it off with a headscarf tied around our necks."

Girls from the 1950s? Got it. "That sounds perfect," I said. This may be one way to get Mom out of wearing the crappy witch costume.

With that figured out, we crossed the street to the theater. Fifty cents to get in and a nickel for a jumbo cherry Charms sucker. Sweet deal. Because of her braces, Vicky couldn't have anything sticky, so she settled on a Hershey's bar.

The movie turned out to be as dumb as some of the TV shows I'd seen in the last couple of weeks. Its one redeeming quality was that it was short. After we walked out of the theater, our eyes adjusting to the sunlight, Vicky tugged on my hand and started running toward the hospital. She wanted to make it to four-o'clock Mass.

Not ten minutes into the service, I figured out why Vicky was so intent on getting there. The hospital priest tore through Mass like there was no tomorrow. We were out the door thirty minutes later.

Back at the house, Grandma was making dinner. Shake 'n Bake Barbeque Chicken, I noted, seeing the box on the countertop. That sounded good.

When the boys came down for supper, Robert looked at me. "Well…?"

"Well, what?" I asked.

"Aren't you going to say, 'It's Shake 'n Bake, and we helped,'" he exclaimed in a pronounced fake Southern accent. I had no idea what he was talking about.

"Isn't that your favorite commercial? Or, is it the Alka-Seltzer commercial where the guy says, 'I can't believe I ate the whole thing.'"

"I'm sick of those." The lie rolled off my lips. I was getting good at this.

"It's about time," said Howard.

Another stellar night on tap at the Connors' house. Did anyone in this family ever get sick of watching TV, or was it just me? First, there was some political comedy called *All in the Family,* followed by *Mary Tyler Moore,* a sitcom about a girl working in a TV studio in Minneapolis.

During *The Bob Newhart Show,* Grandma left the den to make popcorn on the stove. Once each of us kids had a bowl, she poured us cups of orange juice made from frozen concentrate. It was an interesting combination.

Finally, a show came on that appealed to all of us. Together we chuckled at the goofy skits on *The Carol Burnett Show*.

The boys stayed up after that, but I was ready for bed. I had a much better night's sleep than the previous one. Being away from Richard for a day was just what the doctor ordered.

On Sunday, the guys went to church, while me and Grandma slept in. The football game was on at noon, so we ate an early lunch.

After the game, Robert caught me off-guard when he asked if I wanted to play a game with him and Howard. They needed a third person to play *Clue*. We had the new version at home, and I knew how to play, so I agreed to join them.

I got to be my favorite character, Miss Scarlet.

"Professor Plum, in the Billiard Room, with a rope," I shouted when I had all the clues put together. Jumping to my feet, I did a victory dance.

The night got even better when Grandpa made spaghetti and meatballs. It was my favorite meal to start, and *The Betty Crocker Cookbook* version was to die for.

The nature movie featured on *The Wonderful World of Disney* was so-so, but that didn't stop me from watching it. When in Rome, do what the Romans do.

In bed, I thought about the upcoming week, assuming that I'd still be living Mom's life. We'd be sewing our stuffed animals in Home Ec. Friday was a home football game. Saturday was Angela's birthday party. The only thing that I didn't look forward to was dealing with Richard.

My stomach hurt as I thought about it. That dude was really beginning to annoy me. I grabbed Mom's white rosary from her nightstand and made the Sign of the Cross, hoping prayer would take my mind off of things.

"Please, God, let me go back to my life... And if that's not possible at this moment, make Richard stop being mean to me," I prayed. "If you can't do that, can you send him somewhere back in time?" I thought about it for a moment. "Maybe back to the prehistoric days where he can get tormented. By a dinosaur." Just thinking about it brought a devious smile to my face.

Chapter 32

They say God answers all prayers. It's either yes, no or not now. Being the optimist, when I awoke Monday morning to the clanging alarm, I presumed my answer was yes but not quite yet.

It's also been said that you need to pray with your feet. With that in mind, I was determined to stop at the public library on the way back from Home Ec. either Tuesday or Thursday. The building has since been transformed into a museum, but the old location was just a block away from the high school. I wanted to see if I could find any books on time travel so that I could figure out how to get back to my life. Where was a smartphone when I needed one? It'd make this task so much easier.

Thankfully, God deigned to answer one of my prayers. After pleading my case that taking the school year off from piano lessons would benefit both me and the rest of the family, Grandma actually acquiesced and told me I could have a break. Whether it was my rock-solid case or to give her ears and wallet a break, I didn't know, but I was relieved to not have to deal with that.

The week progressed much as I had anticipated a week in Mom's seventh-grade life would go. At school, I did my best to stay clear of Richard, but he did manage to throw some snarky comments my way when he could. My cheeks burned hotter every time he picked on me. He was getting bolder. I did what I could do to put on a brave face but, to be truthful, it was really starting to eat at me.

Every night when I went to bed and thought about the upcoming school day, my stomach killed me. It got to the point that it hurt just to lie down, so I got extra pillows from the hall closet to prop myself upright. It was less painful to fall asleep in a sitting position.

I still hadn't talked to anybody about what was going on. What could they do anyhow? Richard, being the jerk that he was, would probably make them his next target. He wouldn't dare hit a girl, but he had no problem shoving boys around. The one guy that he didn't pick on was Ronald, who was the only person in school bigger and stronger than he was. Unlike Richard, though, that farm boy was a gentle giant.

Thursday after school, I talked Vicky into stopping at the library with me. When I slipped to the desk and asked the librarian if they had any time travel books, she immediately piped up with, "*A Wrinkle in Time.*" *Not going to do the trick. This was real life, not fiction.*

She then suggested that I go through the filing cabinet and search the index cards for topics related to time travel, but that proved to be pointless as well. By the time I figured out the goofy Dewey Decimal System, Vicky was ready to go. It didn't seem like the library had any *Time Travel for Dummies* books anyhow.

When the final bell rang Friday, I let out a sigh of relief. I couldn't wait to get out of the building and put school behind me for the weekend.

Tammy and I met at Vicky's house at six o'clock to do each other's hair. I worked on Tammy's freshly washed hair, pulling the front section to the back of her head and securing it with a ponytail holder. Tammy put Vicky's hair up in a high ponytail and tied maroon and white ribbons around the ponytail holder. Vicky made two braids from the longer section of my hair and tied a different color ribbon on the end of each braid. Mission complete, we walked to the football field.

It was pitch black when the game ended, and the triumphant home fans streamed out of the stadium. To make the trip home shorter, Vicky, Tammy and I cut through the block company. Weaving around countless concrete block porch steps and stoops, we passed a car parked in the lot. We smelled smoke and saw the orange glow of cigarettes dangling from the mouths of three teenage boys sitting inside.

Suddenly, the car engine came to life, the lights flicked on, and the vehicle was put into gear and rolled up behind us.

"Hey chicks, wanna go for a ride?" one of the guys asked out the window.

"No, thanks," said Vicky, staring straight ahead.

"We got booze. Why don't you jump in, and we'll have some fun?"

Holy crap. These guys were creepy. My heart raced. The three of us girls drew closer together and picked up our pace.

"What's the matter? Babies have to get home to your mommies?" asked the driver.

"We're not babies. We're seventh-graders, and

we're not allowed to drink," said Tammy defensively. "And if you're not eighteen, you're not allowed to drink either."

Eighteen?

The guys in the car laughed. "Ooh," said one of them. "We can do what we want, and if you weren't such scaredy cats, you could do what you wanted too."

We picked up our pace, but the vehicle crept after us. When we reached the sidewalk bordering the block company, the car stopped, and the doors opened.

"Run!" shouted Vicky.

We turned left and sprinted down the sidewalk and crossed Beaver Brook.

Car doors slammed. The engine revved.

St. Joseph School loomed in front of us. It was dark but yellow light spilled from the building next door.

"The convent!" I yelled and angled toward the wooden two-story structure. Tammy and Vicky were on my heels as we bounded up the porch steps and pounded on the front door. My heart raced as we anxiously waited for a response. Within seconds, the door opened, and we saw Sister Margaret Mary.

Tires squealed behind us. The three of us girls stumbled through the doorway of the convent and into the foyer. Glancing back outside, we saw the car veer around the corner, the driver shifting it into a higher gear, and then shoot off toward downtown.

Sister Margaret Mary ushered us into the dining

room. Sister Martha and Sister Cecilia walked in with Sister Joan not two steps behind.

"What's the matter, girls?" asked Sister Margaret Mary, concern in her voice.

Shaking and scared half to death, we all spoke at once, trying to tell the story about the boys that were following us.

"Come, come. Let's get you settled down," said Sister Margaret Mary. "Have a seat. Why don't you each take a turn and tell part of the story?"

By then, Sister Joachim joined us.

"The best idea is to stay here for a bit to make sure those boys aren't out there waiting for you," she noted. "They'll lose patience if they don't see you come outside soon."

We nodded in agreement.

Sister Joan stepped forward with a smile on her face. "We were just sitting down to a late supper. Would you girls like to join us for a fish fry?"

The smell of freshly fried fish was too much for any of us to resist. We enthusiastically nodded.

Sister Joan brought in three plates and glasses from the adjoining kitchen. She poured a glass of milk for each of us girls and scooped a couple of fish fillets onto our plates.

The sisters took their seats at the large table, and Sister Margaret Mary led everyone in the meal prayer. As we dug into the fish, Sister Cecilia went to the kitchen. I heard the refrigerator door open. She came back with two Old Milwaukee beers and a bottle opener and proceeded to open the bottles and pour a glass of beer with a frothy head for each of the sisters at the table.

Vicky, Tammy and I gawked at each other in astonishment.

"Sisters drink beer?" I asked in a squeaky voice.

"What's a fish fry without it?" asked Sister Martha.

We stared open-mouthed at her like she'd grown a second head. *Wonder what the kids at school will think when they hear this?*

After we finished eating, Sister Margaret Mary went outside to see if the boys' car was in sight. Seeing nothing, she motioned for us to come to the door and then sent us on our way, promising to keep an eye on us until we were out of her view.

None of us felt like we were out of harm's way yet, so as soon as we got to the next street, we took off, and we didn't stop running until we got to our house. Once I stepped in the back door, Tammy and Vicky scampered off toward their street.

Nasty stitch in my side, I leaned against the wall to catch my breath. I'd never been so happy to see this house in my entire life, no matter what era it was. Once my breathing evened out, I walked upstairs, said a quick goodnight to Grandma, and went down the hall to my room. Without even bothering to brush my teeth, I threw on my nightgown, hopped into bed and covered myself head to toe.

It was a crummy night of sleep. One nightmare after another where people and creatures chased me through town. The next morning, for the first time, I was relieved to wake up to the yellow walls, orange chenille bedspread and lime-green shag carpeting of Mom's old bedroom.

Chapter 33

To be on the safe side, I stuck close to home Saturday morning and early afternoon. I didn't know those boys, but they may know Mom and where she lived. When four o'clock finally arrived, I grabbed the flowered suitcase and my pillow and headed to Vicky's.

Tammy was already there. As we waited for Vicky to finish getting ready, the two of us rehashed what had happened the previous night. We kept our voices low, so Mrs. Holtz couldn't hear us. What if we'd been kidnapped by those guys? Or what if they'd forced us to drink alcohol or smoke? It was scary stuff.

Eventually, Vicky appeared, and we started the six-block trek to Angela's. Connie and Jane got there ahead of us, and shortly afterwards, Patty arrived. We couldn't wait to tell everyone our tale.

Between the girls from St. Joseph's, Angela's twin next-door neighbors, her sister, and Mr. and Mrs. Bergner, four pizzas were gone in no time.

"Okay, girls." Mrs. Bergner clapped her hands together. "It's time for a scavenger hunt."

She pointed to each girl, dividing us into two teams. "You have forty-five minutes to scour the neighborhood to find as many things on this list as you. Each member of the winning team will get a prize. Go!"

Angela, Vicky, Connie, one of the twins, and I took off together. We went door to door, asking neighbors for things like a 4th of July sparkler, a roller skate key, or an S&H Green Stamp. Most of the things were common enough that people had them on hand, but some things were hard to find, like an Indian Head nickel.

"Wait!" I looked up from the list, inspiration coming to me. "My grandpa collects coins."

"Your grandpa?" asked Vicky. "How's that going to help? He doesn't live close by."

"I mean, my dad."

Excitement bouncing from one person to the next, we took off for my house. The other girls camped out in the kitchen to chat with Grandma while I flew upstairs. Rummaging through the top drawer of Grandpa's dresser, a mushy card made me pause. I peeked inside. "Thanks for everything," was written in Grandma Louise's handwriting. This was years before she and Grandpa got married. Was she the reason that Grandma and Grandpa got divorced?

Not having the time — or heart for that matter — to think about it longer, I dropped the card and continued searching for the coin. Finding a leather coin pouch, I dumped out silver dollars and fifty-cent pieces and, thankfully, an Indian Head nickel. Clutching my prize, I raced back downstairs.

The girls said their goodbyes to Grandma, and we ran back to Angela's, arriving with five minutes to spare. We never found a World War II army medal, but the other team couldn't find two of the items, so we won.

Each winner got a set of Clackers. The two balls suspended on a string made a loud clacking noise when the string was yanked up. After hearing us clack those things nonstop, Mrs. Bergner was probably regretting that prize choice.

The homemade chocolate birthday cake with white frosting was amazing. Mrs. Bergner even wrote "Happy 13th Birthday, Angela!" on the cake with icing. The ice cream was from the dairy across from the block company. Vicky and I planned to stop there on the way home from Home Ec. one of these days to get a cone.

After we devoured the cake and ice cream, Angela opened her gifts. She liked the records from me and Vicky and played them right away. The makeup was a hit, and she got some cool jewelry and even a pierced earring stand shaped like a butterfly. Instinctively I felt my earlobes. Thirteen years old and no pierced ears? *That's not acceptable, Mom.*

Angela's sister gave her a Ouija board that everyone oohed and aahed over it. Didn't people know those things are evil? A shiver ran up my spine.

We each took a turn as disc jockey and played records for a while. When it got dark, we strolled through the neighborhood. The braver girls ran up to the houses where boys from our class lived, rang the doorbells and then raced back to hide in the bushes with the rest of us. It was funny watching people come to the door. Some looked confused, and some seemed mad when they discovered that they'd been tricked.

Greg Kohler answered the door when his doorbell

was rung. It was hard not giving ourselves away as we could barely hold our giggles back. After the door slammed shut, we continued on our way, searching for our next victim.

A minute later, footfalls were heard behind us. Turning our heads, we saw a masked man running full force straight at us. We screamed in unison.

The guy stopped, doubling over in laughter as he whipped off the mask. It was Greg.

"Oh, man, if you could've seen the looks on your faces!" He burst out laughing again.

After the initial feeling of relief, some of the girls got mad.

"Greg," yelled Angela, "I almost peed my pants, thanks to you!"

Rather than acting repentant, he guffawed harder. His laughter trailed off as he headed back to his house.

That was enough for us. We called it a night and went back to Angela's to play games. We played several rounds of *Twister.* When Angela unpacked the Ouija board, I took a spot on the far side of the basement to get as far away from it as I could. Maneuvering the handpiece over the board by candlelight and spelling out answers to questions girls posed creeped everyone out. Thankfully, they didn't play long.

I was glad when the lights were flipped back on again. We went to brush our teeth and change into PJs and nightgowns. Spreading ourselves throughout the area, we talked for another hour with girls dozing off one by one. As far as I could tell, I was the last one to fall asleep.

Morning arrived, and we packed up our gear and took off for home. *What a weekend.* And to think, Mom missed it all.

Chapter 34

There were no two ways about it. Mom's life was less-than-amazing. The taunting from Richard was pretty much non-stop. God only knew what his issue was. I certainly couldn't figure it out. There was a crapload of homework every night — which I was now doing, thank-you-very-much. Grandpa — who I was really hoping to get to know better — was hardly ever home. Was he just that busy with bartending, the Elks and bowling, or was he seeing Grandma Louise on the side already?

Howard and Robert, when they weren't ignoring me, were as annoying as heck. As hard as it was to believe — since they were bigger and could push me around — they were even worse than Brock and Brayden. Grandma — when she wasn't working me to death drying dishes, ironing my clothes or pulling weeds from the cracks in the driveway — was hell-bent on killing me with second-hand smoke.

On top of that, trying to maintain Mom's best-friend status with Vicky when Tammy literally lived just steps away from her house was a part-time job in itself.

Mom should be living through this crappola right now, not me. What was it going to take to get me to re-emerge in my own body? If I completely miss my own seventh-grade experience, I'm going to be perturbed, to say the least.

It didn't seem possible that it was already October and close to the end of the first quarter of school. I was beginning to wonder if God even heard my prayers at all.

Thanks to diligently working on Mom's schoolwork every night, as far as I could tell, I was getting good grades. It was hard to say, though. It seems like they didn't use As and Bs in the '70s. You got plus signs and checkmarks indicating working to your ability or falling short. There was a separate mark for participation.

In Home Ec., we finished the stuffed animal project and were in the process of making aprons. Our class completed the first two breakfast units as well. *If I decide to eat anything other than cold cereal for breakfast when I get back to my other life, I'll be in good shape.*

October meant Halloween, which I was looking forward to, regardless of the circumstances. But, it also meant our sex ed unit, which I — and probably almost every other kid in Mom's class — dreaded.

The fateful day came, and Father Laroche took the boys to the library, and Sister Cecilia led the discussion with the girls in homeroom. I couldn't decide what would be worse, hearing Sister lecture on this or Grandma.

"Young ladies," Sister Cecilia said, clapping her hands to get everyone's attention. "Take a slip of paper and write down any questions you may have on your developing bodies or topics related to that. We'll collect the slips in a minute."

There was literally not one thing that I wanted to

ask her. Whatever I needed to know could wait until I got back to my own life. That's what the internet's for.

The first subject on the docket was menstruation. Talk about awkward. My cheeks burned as Sister answered the other girls' anonymous questions on periods. She noted that women who live in community had matching menstrual cycles. *That right there is way more than I want to know.* Eww...

Sorting through the slips, Sister addressed other issues about body odor, proper hygiene and acne. She put one slip back into the basket without reading it aloud. When it was the only one left, she took it out and gave it closer consideration. It had to be the question.

R-iii-nn-gg... The sound of that school bell had never been sweeter. With a look of relief, Sister dumped all the slips into the garbage can and dismissed the class.

Lord only knew what the boys talked about with Father Laroche. Personally, I didn't want to find out.

As horrendous as that class was, any hour away from Richard was a good one. I spent a portion of each day planning strategic ways to avoid him. If that wasn't bad enough, a couple of other guys, thinking the dog thing was done in fun, followed his lead and barked when I was around.

Every third week I had been working in the lunchroom. I would've done it every week if I could have. Eating with the lunch ladies was preferable to having a meal anywhere in the vicinity of Richard.

The days grew colder but, since it hadn't snowed,

we spent every gym class outside. My favorite gym days were the ones that we spent running an obstacle course with Mr. Kovac timing us using a handheld stopwatch.

High school football was winding down. We had the conference championship in the bag. *Monday Night Football* was in full swing.

Grandpa and the boys had their spots staked out for the game the night their team was in the national spotlight. I hurried through dishes and homework so I could join them in the den.

Feet propped on the footstool, Grandpa lay back in his recliner, cradling a Pabst. I took a seat on the glider rocker. The game wasn't going well for our side, and my interest waned the further behind we got.

"What does it mean when the ref puts his hand on his hips?" I asked.

"The player was offsides," said Grandpa, his eyes glued to the TV.

I knew what offsides was in soccer, but not football. "What's that?"

With a sigh, Grandpa explained the call. "The ref is holding his arm across his chest."

"What's that mean?"

"Delay of game. Isn't it time for bed?"

"Not yet."

I watched quietly for another five minutes. "Those guys must really be good athletes," I blurted out.

"Why do you say that?" Grandpa inquired.

"Because the announcer said some of the guys are pro-bowlers. That's pretty cool that they're professional football players and professional bowlers too."

Howard and Robert burst out laughing.

Grandpa shook his head. "To bed, now!" There was no negotiating this one.

I stretched dramatically and stood up. "Goodnight, Daddy. Goodnight, John-Boy. Good night, Jim-Bob."

With that, I left the room, ducking to avoid the couch pillow that Robert threw at my head.

"You don't have to be so cranky. It's just a game!"

Chapter 35

Halloween was here. And so was I. Still. Seeing that this was my second-favorite holiday in the year, I was determined to make the most of it.

With the excitement building for trick-or-treating, it seemed to take forever to get through all of our classes. During recess, Mom's friends made plans for the evening.

Because our house was in one of the nicer neighborhoods, they wanted to start the night there. The group included Bobbi Jo, Connie, Theresa, Tammy and me.

Vicky got stuck taking Charles and Sherry plus Tammy's little sister, who was in Charles' class. Crissy couldn't go because walking got her winded, so Vicky planned to bring a pillowcase to trick-or-treat for her.

Sharon Sanders was going to trick-or-treat for UNICEF. She tried convincing some of us girls to join her, but no one was willing to give up their candy to collect money for charity. Not only that, but Sharon's family lived next to Our Lady of Peace Cemetery, where her dad worked. *Walk by a cemetery on the spookiest night of the year? No, thanks!*

After school, I ran most of the way home so I could get my costume ready. Since Vicky wasn't going with our group, we couldn't be twin '50s girls, but I still liked the costume we'd come up with, so I stuck with it.

It had been a drizzly, rainy day. The rainclouds finally drifted away, but behind them came a cold front. The temperatures were in the high thirties, but that didn't deter us.

By four-thirty, I was dressed in the poodle skirt, Grandpa's white button-up shirt, white knee socks turned down to look like bobby socks, and Grandma's nylon scarf tied around my neck. The finishing touch was her bright red Avon lipstick.

Through the window, I saw Bobbi Jo's brother pull his pickup next to our front curb. I grabbed Grandpa's sweater to complete my ensemble and headed toward the front door.

Grandma took one look at me and stopped me in my tracks. "You're not going out like that."

"Like what?"

"With no coat on. You'll freeze."

"I've got a sweater on. I'll be fine."

"Ally, that's not warm enough. Get your parka from the back closet."

I folded my arms in front of me in frustration. "It's not that cold, and besides, if I cover up my costume, no one will know what I am."

"You're going to catch a cold if you walk around the neighborhood like that for three hours." *Three hours? No wonder kids need pillowcases to collect their loot.* "You're not leaving this house without something warm on."

Grumbling, I relented and grabbed the coat from the back closet. I could always ditch it behind the bushes once I was out of Grandma's sight.

The doorbell rang, making me jump.

"I got it!" Flinging the door open, I saw Bobbi Jo, dressed as a scarecrow. Connie, Theresa and Tammy strode up the sidewalk behind her. I grabbed the pillowcase from the phone bench and headed out the door.

Grandma Schmitt made popcorn balls and caramel apples for each trick-or-treater. Unwrapped treats? That would never fly in my era. The good houses on our block had miniature candy bars or Smarties — superpower pills, as we called them. Peanut butter kisses were doled out at the lame houses.

We ran into Vicky when we got to her neighborhood. The little kids got cold and gave up for the night, so she joined us. I could see why those guys bailed. Even with my coat zipped up to my chin, I was still shivering. Not that I'd admit it to Grandma, but I was glad she'd made me wear the dorky parka.

When the six of us marched up the block behind our house, we hit pay dirt. The Sterlings were giving out full-sized Hershey's bars. It was a first for any of us.

Close to Maple Park, we saw a group of guys running our way. They weren't wearing costumes. Before we knew what was happening, they started spraying shaving cream on us. Shrieking, we ran pell-mell down the block to get away from them. The boys chased us a short distance and then laughed and turned away, presumably to find their next victims.

"Oh, yuk, look at me." Vicky flung her arms out to

display shaving cream stripes up and down the front of her coat.

"I can't believe they did this to us." Connie flung a blob of shaving cream from her pointy black witch hat.

"Let's go home," Theresa said, standing slumped with her pillowcase and mask on the ground by her feet.

"But, it's not eight o'clock yet," Connie said.

"Right!" Tammy bounced on the balls of her feet, a wave of new energy coming from her. "We're not going to let those weirdos make us quit!"

Confident that the coast was clear, we headed in the opposite direction of where the boys went until we got to the next house with its lights on.

"Trick or treat," we yelled in unison.

"Hi, Ally," said the lady at the door. "Aren't you girls cute! It's a bit hard to tell with the jacket, but are you a bobby-soxer?"

I nodded.

"We've got another bobby-soxer and a witch. Is that you, Connie?"

Connie said hello and introduced Bobbi Jo, Theresa, Tammy and Vicky.

"Girls, we ran out of candy twenty minutes ago. But we have some single-serving cartons of orange juice. Would you each like one?"

Heads nodded in agreement. When the lady came back with the small cartons, she put one into each of our pillowcases.

There was oohing and aahing as we walked away. We stopped at a few more houses on that block. With porch lights flicking off, we decided to call it a night and split into two groups to walk home.

Stepping over the front threshold, I kicked off my shoes, dropped my parka on the floor, skipped into the den and dumped the contents of the pillowcase onto the shag carpet to begin sorting.

May as well enjoy the good along with the bad. This was the biggest load of candy I'd ever gotten.

The Hershey's bar got the place of honor at the top of the arrangement, and under that, I lined up the miniature candy bars, Smarties and the other things that I liked. In the spirit of the holiday, I'd give the rest to Howard and Robert.

Assuming that I was going to continue to live in Mom's body for a while, I'd space out eating all the candy. Mom had enough fillings as it was.

The word fillings made me think of the dentist. Mom was scheduled to get braces after the first of the year. I seriously hoped I'd be out of here before then. I'd already gone through that in my own life. Once was enough.

Getting braces would make the Richard situation even more unbearable. *No offense, Mom, but if you'd been a little less dorky, maybe Richard never would have picked on you in the first place. Did you really think this haircut was a good idea? And don't even get me started on these glasses.*

Shaking those thoughts from my head, I concentrated on the project at hand. One hundred and sixty-three pieces. A smile spread across my face. I couldn't wait to dig in.

Chapter 36

Pockets of bright orange and red stood out among the stark trees that had lost their leaves already. Our front, side and backyard required raking every few days.

Jane came over to help me rake on Saturday. Her mom needed leaves to cover their raspberry bushes. Grandpa said he'd give us fifty cents each to rake the whole yard. Apparently, that's the going rate for everything around here. But it was better than nothing.

We raked and bagged the leaves in the back and the side yard first. After two hours of raking, we had a mound of leaves piled up next to the back stoop. Leaves billowed around us as we jumped from the stoop into the massive leaf pile.

After we had our fill of that, we started bagging leaves. I held the garbage bag open as Jane scooped leaves into it. On the last bag, as the leaves filtered over my outstretched arms, I felt something crawling on me. Sucking in my breath, panic rose inside me, and instinctively, I slapped at the hornet hovering on my forearm.

That made it mad, and the next thing I knew, it stung me. *Par for the course in this stupid life.*

The pain brought tears to my eyes. Jane's eyebrows scrunched up with a look of concern. "I'll get your mom."

She bolted up the back steps and into the house. Within a few seconds, Grandma came flying out. "Oh, Ally, I know it hurts," she said, inspecting my outstretched arm. "Let's get you in the house and see if icing it will make it feel better."

I nodded and followed her into the house, Jane one step behind me. Grandma took an ice cube tray from the freezer, pulled back the metal handle to pop some cubes out, and held one on the spot where I'd been stung.

"Feel better?"

"Yes," I said, sniffling.

"Why don't you girls take a break and have a snack?" she offered. "I just baked some brownies. They should be cool enough to eat."

That was one way to brighten my mood. Jane and I sat at the kitchen table, and each had two brownies and a glass of black cherry Kool-Aid. After we finished, the pain diminished. I followed Jane back outside to make leaf houses.

With our rakes, we became architects. Leaf lines were fashioned into walls, rooms and doors. Our elaborate homes had full kitchens, dens, formal living rooms, multiple bedrooms, piano rooms and even sunrooms and greenhouses. Jane and I pretended we were grown up and owned the houses. We talked about our future husbands and our kids.

Seeing that I knew how life actually turned out, not only could I name Mom's future husband but all three of her kids too. As a matter of fact, I knew how things turned out for Jane as well. Not that I would tell her. Let's just say all that music practice paid off.

She was the band director at the high school now.

We took turns touring each other's houses, taking special care to use the doorways and not walk over any walls. Just as we finished, Robert rode into the driveway on his three-speed bike.

"What's up?" he asked.

I proudly showed him my house and pointed out the features in Jane's house.

"Neat pad," said Robert, as he glanced at Jane's work. He then stepped through one of my leaf walls, leaving a trail of leaves behind him.

"I gotta go to the can," he said, continuing to walk through the imaginary walls. "Where is it?"

"Stop it!" I shouted, balling my hands into fists. "You're supposed to use doors to get from one room to the next. You can't just walk through walls."

"Wanna make a bet? Just watch me." He jumped from room to room. "Hey, look, I'm Casper, the friendly ghost."

"Stop it, or I'll tell Mom," I said, my voice rising in anger.

"So, what's new?"

With that, he jumped over the last wall and up the wooden front porch steps and into the house.

"Brothers are so annoying," I said, stamping my foot.

Jane didn't say anything. Maybe she was thinking about her brother with the low draft number.

"We got enough leaves, Jane. Let's go back to your house."

When we got to the Dobransky's, her mom let us go into their garage and each pick out a full-sized candy bar. The memory of the bee sting faded with each bite I took of the Caramello bar. Why couldn't Grandpa have had a vending machine route? That would've been cooler than being an electronics technician and a bartender.

Chapter 37

Sunday was the start of tech week for the school play. The boys stayed after school until almost ten o'clock every night doing the final run-throughs. As much as I wanted to get back to my own life, I'd be okay putting it off for another few days. I was looking forward to seeing *The Fantasticks* after all the work the guys had put into it.

Opening night, Theresa, Connie and I had seats in the fourth row. The show was outstanding. Uncle Howard did an excellent job portraying El Gallo. I'd never seen him on stage before because he'd quit theater after he and his wife started their family. I had no idea how talented he was.

The theme song "Try to Remember" was stuck in my head for weeks. I was still humming it as Thanksgiving Day approached. *Who'd have thought that I'd be living this crazy life for three months, but sure enough, I was.*

As hard as it was to do some days, I had been trying to find something good about each day. Thanksgiving would be the ideal time to focus on what I was grateful for. Who knows, maybe someday I'd look back on this experience and find that it was one of the best things that had ever happened to me.

The four-day weekend coming up was something to be happy about, even if it was just to give me a break from Richard. Just seeing him caused me to tense up, worried that he'd do the dog thing and embarrass me in front of everybody. That, and the fact that his picking on me was starting to get somewhat physical now. He purposely tried tripping me when I walked past his desk, and he'd shove me out of the way with his shoulder if I happened to be in his path.

The popular girls thought it was funny. No surprise there. They were seldom nice to anyone in the not-popular group. One day, Sister Margaret Mary called the entire group to the school office. We found out later that they got chewed out for being mean to their classmates.

I prayed for the day that Richard would be sent to the office for bullying me, but no luck. Thinking about him made my stomach hurt more all the time. There were many days that I didn't want to go to school. The I-don't-feel-good thing didn't fly with Grandma. No puke, no fever, no day off.

When the last bell of the day rang the Wednesday before Thanksgiving, a weight lifted from my shoulders. With no Girl Scout meeting, I sprinted home.

A spicy aroma filled the house. Grandma had spent all afternoon baking. A pumpkin pie and a pecan pie sat cooling on top of the stove. Dinner rolls were rising. Two cans of cranberries, one whole and one jellied, sat on the counter. The turkey was thawing in the refrigerator.

Just like in my normal life, Thanksgiving Day for Mom's family started with the Macy's Thanksgiving Day Parade. Howard's favorite part was the Broadway performances. Robert liked the bands, even if their lip-syncing was terrible. Grandma peeked in from the kitchen every so often to see one of the marching bands. She'd played the clarinet in high school.

At noon the football game came on. Conceding to the guys, Grandma timed everything so we could eat lunch at halftime.

Everyone helped carry plates of food to the table. Grandpa had made his famous stuffing and left out the neck and gizzards so we kids would eat it. There was corn and mashed potatoes and gravy and the cranberries. The star attraction was the turkey, which Grandpa declared weighed more than his bowling ball.

We opted to eat the pies after the game. Grandma and I headed off to start washing the multitude of dishes. After those were finally done, I grabbed the newspaper and knelt down on the den floor to read the comics by the warmth of the heating grate.

Robert sat behind me on the couch. I guess the target was too hard to resist. Out of the blue, he gave me a shove on my rear end with his foot. Unable to catch myself, I fell face forward to the floor.

"Oh, no!" I cried, looking at my crumpled glasses. "They're broken!"

Grandpa snapped the footrest down, bolted out of the recliner, grabbed Robert by the arm and told him to go to his room.

"I can't believe he did that!" I wailed. As Grandma rushed into the den to assess the situation, a thought suddenly occurred to me. *This could be a blessing in disguise.* Maybe I could replace those nerdy things with something less atrocious. "Can I get a new pair tomorrow?" I asked Grandma hopefully.

"We'll bring them to Dr. Knight's Monday morning and order a set of replacement frames."

"Replacement frames? Are you kidding?" My voice rose in frustration. "Can't I just get new ones?"

"Ally, you just got those frames last spring. It's less expensive to replace the frames and keep the lenses. They're not damaged."

"I hate these frames!"

"You didn't hate them when you picked them out," Grandma shot back. "You're stuck with them now. Maybe when you're in high school, you can update them."

Teeth clenched, I asked, "How long will it take to get new frames?"

"I would imagine about two weeks."

"Two weeks? What am I supposed to do until then?"

"There's electrical tape in Dad's toolbox. We'll tape them up until the new ones get here. As long as you're careful, they should stay together."

In essence, for the next two weeks, I'd look like the dork in Mom's *Mystery Date* game. As if I didn't have enough stuff to worry about. Richard would have a field day with this one.

Grandma took the broken glasses to start the repairs. The football game was over, but I'd lost my appetite. The decision was made to save the pies for later. Grandpa called Robert down, made him apologize, and then told us to grab our jackets.

A bowling ball bag in each of his hands tipped me off to the next item on the Connors' family agenda. Bowling must be what families do on Thanksgiving Day if they don't have relatives to visit.

Much to Grandpa's chagrin, I hit more gutters than pins, but the bowling was relatively fun, and it took my mind off my broken glasses. No one there mentioned anything. Doubt I'd have that much luck at school Monday.

Chapter 38

The day after Thanksgiving was Robert's birthday. Still upset with him, I didn't even sing as Grandpa lit the fifteen candles on his birthday cake.

My mood improved a bit when Grandma handed me a wrapped gift. Apparently, it was tradition in their house that when one child had a birthday, the other kids each got one gift as well. Why hadn't Mom carried that tradition on? I'd be totally cool with that. A snowman with a bright pink scarf and matching hat and mittens nestled in an Avon box. It was a pin, and the middle section opened up to reveal Sweet Honesty rub-on perfume. It smelled so good. I pinned it on my shirt and wore it for the rest of the weekend.

Monday came around, whether I was ready for it or not. It didn't take long for Richard to spot me when I got to school. Not that it hurt less, but at least I was prepared for the barrage of comments he threw my way.

The first Sunday of Advent, Grandpa and the boys trekked to the used car lot on the edge of town to buy a Christmas tree. Grandma and I decorated the house while they were gone.

We Scotch-taped a plastic picture of Santa to the front door that made it look like he was walking into our house. Holly branches and Christmas knickknacks lined the bookshelves in the dining room. The set of Three Wisemen that Grandma handcrafted had a place of honor on the lowest shelf.

Stockings were hung near the feet of the wisemen. The fuzzy red fur socks with matching white fake fur trim had our names printed on them in glitter. A skinny elf with bendable arms and legs stuck out of each stocking.

The guys returned home, their faces red from the cold, dragging a chunky tree into the living room. Grandpa poured himself a glass of whiskey to warm up.

His job was to string lights on the tree. He set about testing each strand of lights to make sure all the big colorful bulbs would light up. With those old sets, if one light was burned out, they all went out, so he had to take each bulb out one at a time to find the culprit.

This process took longer than it would actually take to string the lights on the tree. I watched Grandpa working away on his hands and knees, sipping from his glass every so often saying, "God bless it," when he couldn't figure out which bulb was the bad one. By the time the lights were all aglow, he'd downed two full glasses of whiskey.

Grandma wasn't happy with him. They got into an argument, and Grandpa stormed out of the house. In tears, Grandma ran up to her bedroom. The boys went their separate ways as well. It was such an uncomfortable situation. Not knowing what else to do, I attempted to string the lights on the tree myself.

What was supposed to be one of the most fun days of the year turned into a bust. How did Mom handle her life? Sure, there were good times, but she had to go through so much crap. And now that she'd skipped town, I was the one who had to deal with everything.

Wanting to reclaim the Christmas spirit, I listened to a Bing Crosby album as I worked. The finished product was less-than-amazing, but it was done. Snagging ornaments one at a time, I placed them onto the tree with little wire hooks. That done, I arranged a red felt skirt under the tree.

By then, it was dark outside, the only light coming from the colorful bulbs. Glasses off, I admired my work. Without glasses, everything was fuzzy, and light radiated from each bulb.

The four of us ate dinner in silence, waiting for Grandpa to return. An hour later, snow began to fall. Not long after that, Grandpa finally walked in the back door. I slowly let out the breath that I'd been holding the whole time he was gone.

With snow on the ground the next morning, Grandma made me wear snow pants and boots to school. Thankfully, she'd finally relented and let me get a new jacket to replace Mom's parka. Goodbye, Eskimo Mom. Hello, snow bunny.

I'd spotted the ideal coat at Louise's Clothing Store a couple weeks before. It was a white ski jacket with contrasting tan and black inserts and matching black ski pants. Mom would thank me the next time she went to Pine Hill skiing.

Grandma wasn't excited about the ski outfit because it was white and would show all the dirt, it was thin and wouldn't keep me warm, and it was expensive in her eyes. I don't know about her, but forty-five dollars was a bargain to me.

Regardless of her misgivings, there was no swaying me. If I had to live this crappy life for an extended period of time, the least I deserved was some decent clothing. I used every negotiating skill in my arsenal until I got Grandma to say yes to the purchase.

The next day at school, I felt like a boss wearing something that no one else owned for once.

Other than the fact that it was still 1974, December was off to a pretty good start. Even if I still prayed every night to be transported back to my life, I decided that I would make the best of my favorite month of the year, whatever year that happened to be.

The school hallways were cheerily decorated, we worked on Christmas worksheets and Christmas art projects, and we got homemade Christmas candy for dessert at lunchtime.

Christmas music played everywhere. Grandma had it on nonstop at the house, it was piped into the stores downtown, and we practiced singing Christmas carols for Midnight Mass twice a week.

I was even dreaming about those Christmas songs. At least it was a break from the nightmares I'd been having. Nothing worse than waking up in the middle of the night with a pounding heart and aching stomach.

When St. Nick's Eve arrived, I eagerly ran to check out my stocking. Digging in, I discovered a candy bar and a *Richie Rich* comic book. The boys seemed more enthusiastic about their stuff than I was. Seeing that

Howard eventually had a career as a comic book artist, it made sense.

The second Tuesday in December was the downtown Christmas Parade. Our Girl Scout troop constructed a float. Basically, a cardboard train, called the Holiday Express, pulled on a hay wagon that was hooked to a pickup truck.

Some girls rode on the float, and the rest of us, dressed like elves, walked alongside the float and threw Tootsie Rolls to the kids lining the route.

The parade began on the west end of Main Avenue by the football field, went to Mueller Hardware Store and ended in the parking lot across from The American Legion. In addition to the half-dozen floats, there was the fire truck, a group of horses with Miss Teenage Rodeo leading the way, Boy Scouts marching with a giant American flag clutched in their hands, the mayor escorting his wife, and, at the tail end, Santa Claus in a horse-drawn sleigh.

Dark clouds rolled in just as the parade began. We hadn't gone more than two blocks when it started to pour. Getting soaked was bad enough. Being wet and freezing made it completely miserable. Our fingers were frozen, making it hard to throw candy to the kids.

One thing about parades, there was no speeding them up. It took forever to get to the Legion. From there, we ran back to St. Joseph's and tumbled in the side door. A few steps into the building, my glasses steamed up. *Sure would be nice to have contacts again. I wonder what it would take to talk Grandma into those?*

Mrs. Caruso was waiting for us in the cafeteria with hot chocolate and Christmas cut-out cookies. I wrapped both hands around the Styrofoam cup, happy to thaw my fingers. By the time everyone finished their snack, moms and dads were coming into the building to collect their kids.

Note to self. Do not ever volunteer to be in a parade again. Or, at least, a winter parade.

Chapter 39

When the bell rang Friday after school, I ran the whole way home so I could dib the front seat of the car. Grandpa was taking me and the boys to the city to go Christmas shopping.

There was no snack waiting because Grandma had started a part-time job at Robinson's Jewelry working Friday nights and Saturday afternoons. She loved jewelry and got a discount. Seemed like a good fit for her. Maybe now she'd finally get up the nerve to have her ears pierced.

When the boys got home, we took off right away. Forty-five minutes later, we pulled into the parking lot at a McDonald's.

"I'll take a cheeseburger, just ketchup, a small fry and a vanilla milkshake," I told Grandpa.

The boys both turned around and stared at me.

"Very funny," said Grandpa. "If you want a cheeseburger, you're getting the works. We're not waiting for them to make a special order."

Isn't the food made to order? Even if it wasn't, would it really be that hard to wait an extra five minutes to have what I wanted?

"Fine," I said, "I'll just have a large fry and a vanilla milkshake."

After everyone finished their food, we headed downtown to Prange's Department Store. Standing in front of the building, we admired the window displays. Each one was different, but they all showcased brightly lit Christmas trees and mechanical figures that moved or danced. One window depicted a scene from *The Nutcracker.*

If it hadn't been freezing, I would've stayed out there longer, but after ten minutes, even with Mom's chunky moon boots on, I couldn't take the cold anymore. We entered the building together and headed towards the escalator.

Santa's workshop was on the second floor. The boys wanted to go up there to see more of the animated stuffed animals and the elaborate Christmas trees on display. They were as into Christmas as Mom was.

Agreeing to meet at eight forty-five by the entrance with the big snow-flocked Christmas tree, we split up. Grandpa headed to the beauty area to get perfume for Grandma, and then he intended to go to the kitchen section to get a pressure cooker, whatever that was.

My job would be to wrap the gifts he bought before Christmas. Assuming I was still around. I liked wrapping gifts as much as anybody, but I'd still rather be back in my own life.

From what I gleaned talking to Robert, the kids bought gifts for each other and for Grandma and Grandpa too. I had a list of ideas with me.

Grandpa always carried a cloth hankie in his back pocket. He'd probably appreciate some new ones. The men's department featured monogrammed hankies. I grabbed a box with the letter C for Connors embroidered in the corner of each one.

Since Grandma wore scarves every day, I went to the ladies' accessory department next. *Orange paisley? The epitome of '70s modern chic. Perfect.*

Next on my list was Robert. He'd be playing tennis in the spring, so a tube of bouncy, fluorescent yellow tennis balls would do the trick. I had a limit of two dollars per gift. That made Howard's gift harder to determine. He liked sweets as much as I did, so I headed back up the escalator to the candy department. A half-pound of fruit jelly candy and chocolate-covered raisins later, his gift was good to go.

Vicky and I were exchanging gifts too, so I headed to the juniors' department next. Rainbow-striped knee-high toe socks seemed to be in style, so I grabbed a pair. Then I went to the cosmetic area and bought a root beer-flavored Lip Smackers to complete the gift.

With everything paid for and tucked in a Prange's bag, I walked around both floors of the store, riding the escalator a couple more times, and then made my way to our assigned meeting place. Grandpa was there already. Howard came up behind us, but there was no sign of Robert. We waited ten minutes, Grandpa getting crabbier by the minute. Finally, he told me and Howard to stay put and started checking the other entrances.

Sure enough, he discovered Robert by another door with a similar Christmas tree. Back together once again, we left the store and marched to the parking lot. It was a silent trip back home.

Life is certainly going to get a lot less complicated for these people when they finally invent cell phones.

Chapter 40

I couldn't have been happier when school got out the Friday before Christmas. Two whole weeks without having to worry about Richard. If, by some weird chance, I was still here in January, maybe he'd be bored with me and would find someone else to torment.

A Charlie Brown Christmas was on that night. I'd seen it a hundred times, but I sat down and watched it with Howard and Robert. Afterwards, they accompanied me to the high school for the basketball game.

The next day, Connie, Theresa and I spent most of the afternoon playing in the newly fallen snow. Sunday was church and the football game. On Monday, I relaxed, read and counted down the hours until Christmas Eve arrived.

Tuesday was a busy day. Grandma had made Christmas cutout cookies over the weekend and stored them in a big green Tupperware container. Us kids were assigned to decorate them.

We formed an assembly line around the kitchen table. Grandma mixed powdered sugar and water in the gold mixing bowl. A large sheet of wax paper lay in front of each decorator. In the middle of the table stood two shaker bottles of colored sugar and a plastic container of Red Hots and one with edible silver balls that looked like tiny steely marbles. Red, yellow, blue and green food coloring bottles were at the ready for small batches of colored frosting.

Once the white frosting was mixed, Grandma let us go to work. We had our choice of cut-outs to work on: a reindeer, gingerbread man, bell, star, Christmas tree or Santa. Taking one of each, I spread white frosting on the cookie and then sprinkled it with either red or green sugar.

Robert's cookies were more elaborate. He spread a base of either red or green frosting on each one, used different sugar colors and added steelies and Red Hots for the finishing touch.

Howard outdid us all. He only decorated gingerbread men and each cookie became a different superhero. There was Batman, Robin, Spiderman, Superman, The Green Hornet, and other characters that I didn't recognize.

His newest comic books in front of him for reference, Howard putzed around for forty-five minutes, creating his masterpieces. I decorated four dozen cookies in half the time.

Cookie project complete, I hurried through my bologna and margarine sandwich so I could wrap the Christmas gifts hidden in my dresser drawer.

The tennis balls were hard to wrap because the container wasn't square, but the gifts for the rest of the family were easy enough to wrap. When the last gift tag was applied, I put the wrapping supplies in the hallway so Howard and Robert could use them later.

Vicky and I had arranged to meet at her house at four o'clock. It was getting dark, and snow fell as I strolled over there. The Holtz's had a one-story house, but it had a cathedral ceiling in the living room. An immense tree stationed there was visible from the sidewalk as I approached their house.

When I got there, Charles, Sherry and Crissy were being ushered out the door. Mr. and Mrs. Holtz were taking them to four-thirty Mass. Vicky was going to midnight Mass with us. This created the ideal time for Vicky and me to exchange gifts without an audience.

Settled in front of their Christmas tree, Vicky opened her gift first and smiled when she saw the toe socks.

"These are so cool, Allison. Thank you!"

"You're welcome," I replied. "There's one other gift in the box."

"Root beer! I love that flavor," exclaimed Vicky, uncapping the Lip Smackers and applying some to her lips. She then reached under the tree and grabbed a tall, skinny box.

Once the gold foil paper was off, I opened the top and saw layers of tissue paper. At the very bottom of the box sat a little brown ceramic mouse. He held a tiny book of Christmas carols in his paws, and his mouth was open like he was singing.

"Oh, Vicky! He's adorable!" I couldn't believe my eyes. All these years later, Mom still had him in one of our boxes of Christmas decorations. Until this moment, I'd had no idea where it had come from.

A half-hour later, I was back at home. It was steamy warm in the kitchen when I arrived. Grandma was spooning food into serving dishes.

"When I walk through a room, let them see you

love me...” sang Grandma along to a record as she worked.

“When you come home at night, take me in your arms and hold me, and kiss me, and say you love me, love me...love me.... That’s what I want for Christmas.”

Not the cheeriest Christmas song by any means. She seemed to like it, though.

“Ally, can you come here once?”

No, I think I’ll come here twice, I thought sarcastically.

“Sure, just let me put my coat away,” I said dutifully as I hung my coat on the hook in the closet and stepped back into the kitchen. “Yah?”

“Can you get out the plates and nice glasses and set the dining room table?”

“The Looney Toons glasses from A&W?”

“No. Real glasses. It’s a holiday.”

“All right,” I said, skipping to the cabinet.

Everyone was in a good mood at dinner. Grandpa made Tom and Jerrys afterwards with watered-down versions for us kids. Grandma even indulged and had one too.

The five of us spent the evening in the den watching Christmas shows. We laughed at the skits on *The Perry Como Christmas Show* as we munched on cookies. When it was over, we placed a couple of undecorated cookies on a tray for Santa — who allegedly didn’t care for frosted cookies when he stopped at the Connors’ house — and put it on the end table in the living room.

After the ten o'clock news, everyone went upstairs to dress up for church, including Grandma. By quarter-to-eleven, we were ready to go. Stepping out into the cold night, we were engulfed in silence, our path to the garage lit by the moon and about a million stars overhead. Gazing at the breathtaking view overhead, it was easy to imagine that it was Christmas Eve in my own life. Steam billowed out of my mouth as I heaved a deep-felt sigh.

When we pulled into Vicky's driveway, the back-porch light flashed, so we knew someone saw us. After waiting two minutes, Grandpa made me get out of the car and knock on the door. Mrs. Holtz said Vicky was brushing her teeth and would be right there. Another two minutes passed, and she finally came to the door, pulling her coat on and shoving her feet into her shoes without bothering to tie them.

All four of us kids scrunched into the backseat of the car for the six-block drive to St. Joseph's. We filed into the church through the side door. Grandpa, Grandma and the boys went to the pew on the left-hand side of the church that we always sat in. Vicky and I went down the side aisle to the back of the church and climbed the stone steps to the choir loft.

There were a half-dozen kids from our class hanging their coats on the back of the folding metal chairs surrounding the organ when we got up there. Twelve seventh-graders were in the choir: me, Vicky, Connie, Tammy, Stacey, Rebecca, Jane, Rhonda, Jonathon Ruzek, Greg and Kurt Bradford.

Sister Joan perched on the bench facing the organ, looking over her sheet music. Vicky and I took off our coats and sat in the seats farthest to Sister's, right in the second row. Jonathon took the chair next to us.

He combed the blond bangs off his forehead and pushed up his wire-framed glasses and, in an uncharacteristic move, initiated a conversation.

"Me and my sister got to open up our gifts before church tonight," said Jonathon.

"Really?" I said. "Get anything cool?"

"My big gift was an electronic football game."

"Neat," I replied. "My brother Robby got that for his birthday in November. You're gonna like it."

"I got this too," he said, holding his left hand out.

A silver ring encasing a smooth oval stone shone from his finger.

"A mood ring?" Vicky's eyes lit up. "Cool. I asked for one for Christmas too."

It seemed like a strange gift for a guy, but there was something intriguing about it. Throughout the night, I couldn't stop glancing at it. The colors changed from dark blue to aqua and, at one point, yellow. I wondered what that said about Jonathon's mood.

The highlight of Mass was singing "Do You Hear What I Hear?" as the organ music pounded in my chest. "Oh, Holy Night," was great too, even if Kurt couldn't stay on key. He'd been a soprano when rehearsals began two months ago. Now his voice switched octaves every other line.

Heads bobbed as Mass went along, especially during Father Laroche's homily. Everyone in the choir came to attention when we had a response to sing. The recessional song, “Joy to the World,” gave the girl sopranos a chance to shine. After weeks of practice, we finally got to sing the descant in public for the first time. Our voices raised above the melody and sounded amazing. I couldn’t stop humming it after church.

Once Vicky was safely home, we drove the block back to our house, snowflakes illuminated by the street lights guiding the way.

After four days of not having to deal with Richard, my stomach finally stopped hurting. Moments after sliding into bed, I was sound asleep.

Chapter 41

Six hours later, I bolted upright in bed. Didn't matter whose life I was in at the moment. *It's Christmas!*

Excitement and anticipation racing through me, I scurried down the hall, knocking on Robert and Howard's doors as I went.

"Wake up!"

Without waiting for a response, I skipped down the stairs.

With the Christmas tree plugged in, I noticed something in my Christmas stocking. Grabbing it off the hook, I took a seat on the carpet, dumped it out and two unwrapped Avon boxes tumbled to the floor.

Mom's going to love this! The smaller box held a lip-shaped compact that opened to reveal two lip gloss compartments. Frostlight Peach and Frostlight Pink, according to the label. Dipping my pinky into the pink lip gloss, I applied it to my lips using the little mirror in the compact as a guide.

A puppy cologne decanter sat nestled in the bigger box. Princess of Yorkshire Sweet Honesty Cologne. The same scent as the snowman pin. It was adorable.

Something was wedged in the heel of the Christmas stocking. I inserted my hand in it and pulled out a pair of knee-high orange-and-yellow-striped toe socks. Mom and Vicky could be twins when she got back. *Nifty!*

The boys lumbered into the dining room and grabbed their stockings from the shelf. Howard dumped his out and found art pencils, a gummy eraser and a pack of football cards. Robert got a deck of magic cards and a pack of guitar picks.

Slippered feet shuffled down the steps. Grandma and Grandpa were up. I raced into the kitchen to start the coffee. That done, we all gathered around the tree to open the wrapped gifts.

Youngest kid privilege meant I got to be Santa's helper. At least there's one advantage to living Mom's life. Gifts were handed out and opened one at a time, all eyes on the recipients.

Grandpa got his hankies, a tie, new pajamas and a pack of golf balls. Probably the same stuff he got every year, but he was good at acting surprised each time he unwrapped a gift. Grandma knew most of what she was getting since Grandpa treated her wish list like a grocery shopping list, but she still managed to ooh and aww over the gifts from our family and her relatives back home.

Howard and Robert each got a couple of albums. Howard's were Broadway show soundtracks. Robert got Paul McCartney and Wings and John Denver. The gift that he was most excited about was the spiral-bound guitar music book with the top hits from the 1970s.

Us kids all got clothes too. I'd dog-eared the pages in the J.C. Penney catalog marking items that I thought Mom would like. Grandma came through with flying colors. Teal-colored corduroys with a striped cowl-neck sweater to match. The epitome of '70s chic in my eyes.

Three new *Nancy Drew* books were added to Mom's collection. The best gift of all was a bracelet Grandma bought with her discount at Robinson's. Two strands of silver metal connected to an oval centerpiece; the word Allison engraved on it in cursive. Surprisingly, I didn't recognize it. So pretty and dainty. I couldn't imagine Mom would have ever gotten rid of it.

The last gift I opened was a one-year diary. *Perfect!* When Mom gets reunited with her body, she'll know what she missed while she was gone.

With the Christmas tree skirt empty, Grandpa stepped behind the couch and pulled out a pair of skis for me and a set for Robert. I was super excited about those. I'd been snowboarding at Pine Hill for years. I doubted that I'd still be here after the first of the year, but, if by some weird chance I was, it would be cool to learn to ski.

Howard waited expectantly for Grandpa to present him with his big gift, but Grandpa settled back onto the couch without a word.

A thought came to me. Was it possible that the calculator I'd found in the bathroom closet a couple months ago was a gift for Howard? What was the best way to bring this up, so Grandma and Grandpa didn't know that I was snooping?

"Thanks for all the gifts, everybody! Everything's great," I said enthusiastically.

"I spent weeks and weeks shopping," said Grandpa. "It was a lot of hard work." That joke — in his eyes — never grew old. He was still saying it. We all knew that the grandmas bought the majority of the gifts.

"The skis are cool. Did you get them at Mueller's Hardware?" I asked, even though I figured as much.

"I did. Saw Laura's dad when I was there but didn't get a chance to talk to him. Busy this time of year."

"I suppose. So, you got my gift and Robert's gift there. Neat."

Grandpa pursed his lips together. "Hold on. Forgot something." He made a beeline for the downstairs bathroom. A minute later, he was back, holding something behind him.

"Not wrapped, but I hope you like it, Howard." He held out the Texas Instruments box. Howard's face lit up, and he caught the box when Grandpa tossed it to him. Opening it up, he pulled out a black calculator. He smiled from ear to ear.

"Watch this." Howard punched a couple numbers and turned the calculator upside down. Robert burst out laughing. I looked over Howard's shoulder and saw four, three, seven, seven. From the opposite view, it spelled out the word hell. Howie jammed the C button to clear the display before Grandpa could see it.

With all the gifts accounted for, Grandma gathered the wrapping paper, wadded it up and walked to the kitchen to throw it away. At that point, everyone grabbed their gifts and deposited them in their rooms. Grandma never was one for clutter.

We went our own ways from there. Howard stayed in his room to listen to his new albums, Robert grabbed his guitar and went to the den to work on some songs, Grandma took a seat at the dining room table to write out thank you notes, and Grandpa lay back on the couch reading his new elephant joke book that the boys got him.

I hunkered down and read *The Mystery of The Tolling Bell.* It was the best day I'd had since I'd taken over Mom's life. *If only every day could be like Christmas.*

Chapter 42

Not sure how Mom would have rated it, but, regardless of the circumstances, it was one of the best Christmas vacations I'd ever had. No stomach aches, no worrying about Richard, time to sleep, read and play outside in the snow.

A couple times, Mom's friends and I walked to Muck Pond to sled after lunch. Vicky's dad gave us large sheets of plastic that had covered rolls of carpet at his store. We used them to slide down the hill that led to the swimming pond. Some people had toboggans, but the majority of the kids had makeshift sleds like ours.

The neighborhood surrounding Maple Park had a ton of kids back then. Everybody streamed over to the park at night to play *Red Rover* and *Crack the Whip*. For *Red Rover*, kids divided into two even teams lined up on opposite sides of the ice. Team members held hands and called out, "Red Rover, Red Rover, send so and so over." The kid who got called skated full speed towards the other team, attempting to break through the line. If they broke through, they got to take back one of the two people whom they had gotten between. The poor people who couldn't break through usually ended up flat on their backs on the ice. Once they were on their feet again, they joined that team. The game ended when all the people were on one side of the ice.

If that wasn't dangerous enough, then there was

Crack the Whip. It was fun when you were in the middle but dangerous being on the end. Everyone held hands and formed a line. The lead person zigzagged back and forth across the ice, gaining speed as they went. At some point, the people on the tail end flew off into the snowbanks.

One day a group of us girls went to River Park to skate. It was further away, but it had a warming shelter. We could wear our boots there and change into our skates rather than killing our ankles walking in them.

Sister Martha met us there. Who knew that sisters could skate? The biggest surprise was seeing her don white figure skates. All her other footwear — from her shoes to her galoshes — was black.

On New Year's Eve, Vicky had to watch Charles, Sherry and Crissy. Mrs. Holtz said that she could have a sleepover while she babysat. I was more than happy to get the invitation. Even though Vicky and Tammy had been hanging out, it looked like I was still in first place in the best-friend race.

With Grandpa at the supper club tending bar and the boys heading off to parties, it was going to be a quiet night around our house. I'm sure Grandma would appreciate that. She seemed to like her alone time.

Because Howard had that party, he asked me if I would listen to WWKA when they counted down the top one hundred songs of the year and keep track of the top twenty for him. Wanting to end the year on a positive note and hoping to build up his relationship with Mom a bit, I agreed to do it.

My breath fogged the air on the walk over. I zipped my ski jacket as high as it would go and quickened my pace. Knocking, then entering the back door, I could make out the kids finishing their dinner through my fogged glasses. Mr. and Mrs. Holtz were running late, so they gave each of their kids a quick hug and a kiss and scurried past me and out the door.

I tidied up the kitchen while Vicky helped the girls get their teeth brushed and their nightgowns on. After Charles put on his pajamas, everyone sat near the Christmas tree, and Vicky pulled out a stack of games.

The kids loved *Ants in the Pants.* Four rounds later, we switched to *Trouble.* Crissy was too little to play by herself, so she took a seat on my lap, and we partnered up. She was really growing on me. I'd never really been into kids, but if I could have some as cute as her, I'd be open to the concept of being a mom someday. Protectively, I hugged her little body.

Next up was making pictures with the *Light Bright* set. Despite her health issues, Crissy had good fine-motor skills and knew all her colors. She grasped the pegs with her blue-tipped fingers and inserted them into the proper spots to follow the pattern. The kids created the picture of a snowman holding a shovel as a surprise for their mom and dad.

With a promise to keep the *Light Bright* plugged in until their parents got home, the kids marched off to their rooms in the rear section of the house.

That taken care of, Vicky and I returned to the kitchen and turned the radio up. Grabbing the notebook that I'd brought, I sat down just in time to jot down song twenty, "Hooked on a Feeling."

Mr. Holtz had picked up a frozen pizza for us. We preheated the oven, took the pizza out of the freezer and put it on a cookie sheet to bake. Vicky dug through their cabinet for some chips.

Grabbing the Doritos bag, we both looked at it in surprise. "Are you serious?" Vicky grumbled, holding up the blue and white bag. "I specifically told him to pick up the Nacho flavor. I can't believe he messed this up."

"Any other bags up there?" I asked, hopefully.

"No."

"At least he tried," I said, defending Mr. Holtz as I thought again about his fate and how much Vicky would probably miss him when he was gone. "And some chips are better than no chips. Let's have some while the pizza bakes."

Vicky agreed and tugged the bag open. We each reached in and grabbed a chip. *Now I can see why Vicky was complaining so much. Talk about bland.*

Every three or four minutes, I grabbed my pen and jotted down the name of the next song on the list. "Sunshine on My Shoulders" by John Denver — Father Dom's lookalike — was number eighteen.

Vicky and I talked about Christmas, school and things she was looking forward to in the upcoming year. The one topic that we didn't broach was Richard. It was pretty obvious that everyone knew that He Who Must Not Be Named had it out for me, but no one ever said anything in my defense. *What's up with that?*

If this wasn't a temporary situation — which I still

prayed it was — I'd confide in somebody. Not sure who, but there'd have to be a sympathetic person somewhere. Maybe Mom had a better way of handling this than I did. A sigh escaped my lips. *What I wouldn't give to be able to talk to her now.* I didn't usually seek out her advice — and wasn't all that receptive to it when she offered it unsolicited — but I'd sure love to tap into her life experience and wisdom now.

Vicky and I scarfed down the entire pizza. We took our glasses of soda into the living room — *God forbid that Mrs. Holtz ever finds out* — and sat in the darkened room by the tree.

I plugged the radio into the living room socket just in time to hear song nine, "Bennie and the Jets." *Holy cow, Elton John has been around forever.*

Not wanting to disappoint Howard, I kept writing songs down, even when I was sick of the project. After a while, we turned the radio volume down a bit and watched *New Year's Eve Rockin' Eve.*

Continuing our conversation, we talked about how neat it would be to be the big men on campus at St. Joseph's next year as eighth-graders. Hopefully, that will be Mom's experience, not mine. We talked about the kids in our class, figured out a weekend to ski at Pine Hill, and discussed why eighth-grade boys were infinitely cooler than seventh-grade boys.

As it neared eleven o'clock our time, a guy pointed to the oversized disco ball ready to drop. My heart beat faster. Maybe I was only scheduled to be in Mom's body until the end of 1974, and I'd be transported back into my own body at the stroke of midnight. Eastern time, Central time, it was good either way.

Grabbing our glasses, Vicky and I counted backwards from ten to one as the ball descended. As the people in New York City celebrated, we yelled "Happy New Year" and clinked our glasses together.

Body still intact, I turned off the TV just as a picture of a flag came on and the "Star-Spangled Banner" played, signaling the end of the broadcast day. We went back to chatting and listening to the radio. Nearing midnight, an instrumental song took spot number three. As it wound down, the opening notes of "Seasons in the Sun" played.

"If they're playing this song now, that means it's number two," I noted. "Are there any good songs left?"

"They played 'The Loco-Motion' already, right?" asked Vicky.

"That was number six," I said, perusing my list.

"Then I have no idea what the top song is."

We listened intently for the opening notes of the next song.

"'The Way We Were?'" It was the theme song from a movie that I'd seen with Grandma. It had such a dumb ending that I couldn't stand the song. What girl would ever leave Robert Redford? He was a stud back in the day.

"I can't believe we waited up until midnight to hear this," Vicky crabbed.

"Me, either." *Hopefully, this isn't a bad omen.*

Chapter 43

Bad omen it was. I didn't magically convert back into the old me when I woke up on New Year's Day. On top of that, 1975 was off to a crummy start.

The first day back to school, I wasn't in the building more than five minutes before I had my first confrontation with Richard.

"Get a new leash for Christmas, dog?"

That guy annoyed the crap out of me, but with no snappy comeback, I just crossed to the other side of the room. The goal once again was to keep as much space as humanly possible between me and him. I didn't want him talking to me, and I didn't want him touching me in any way, shape or form.

During Music, something skimmed my shoulder and landed on the floor in front of me. I reached to pick up the paper football but then stopped, realizing where it most likely came from. A glance over my shoulder confirmed my suspicion.

Richard smirked at me behind his hand. Keeping his eyes on me, he leaned over, said something to Eric Masterson, and they both broke out in laughter.

I took a breath to steel myself against his antagonizing. Avoiding Richard seven hours a day, five days a week, was next to impossible. We had every...single...class together.

"Richard, may I speak with you please?" My ears

perked up. Sister Joan motioned for Richard to approach the piano bench. They were close enough that I could hear every word between them.

"I appreciate your efforts in choir, Richard," said Sister in a hushed voice. "However, everyone is blessed with different talents. Unfortunately, I don't think singing is one of yours."

Richard's face registered no emotion as she continued. "I contacted the band director, and he said they have an opening in the percussion section. You'll be starting band on Wednesday. The drums may be a good fit for you."

"Okay, I guess," Richard mumbled in reply.

I bit my lip to stop the whoop that threatened to burst out of me. *A reprieve two afternoons every week?* Just thinking about it, the constant restriction in my chest loosened considerably.

After that bright spot, however, the rest of January was one dark day after another. My only hope was for a snow day. I watched the weather every night until the magic word blizzard was finally uttered by the weatherman. Clutching the decorative pillow from the couch to my chest, I pleaded, "Oh please, oh please, oh please."

At the crack of dawn the next morning, I jumped out of bed and ran to my window. Scraping frost from the glass with my fingernail, I saw a ton of snow outside. Our driveway wasn't even visible. Bounding to the dresser, I clicked on Mom's transistor radio. The announcer listed, in alphabetical order, the cities with school closings.

Finally, hearing the name of our town, I turned off

the radio and ran to tell the boys.

I went to Robert's room first, knocked and then flung the door wide open. "There was a blizzard last night. We have a snow day!"

"Cool," he replied. He turned over to go back to sleep.

Howard didn't even use words. Just grunted and pulled the covers over his head.

Next, I knocked on Grandma and Grandpa's door.

"Come in," said Grandma.

Opening the door a crack, I noticed that Grandpa's bed was made. He must've left early for the base.

"School's canceled today."

"Are you sure?" she asked in a sleepy voice.

"I just heard it on WWKA."

"Oh, then it must be true. Why don't you go back to bed before you wake yourself up more?"

Too late for that. Wide awake, a whole day in front of me and no Richard to contend with? *It doesn't get much better than that.*

Grabbing my robe, I slipped downstairs. The streetlights highlighted the heavy snow cascading to the ground. The flakes were pretty in the dim light, but the howling wind made me glad to be inside.

I took out a cereal bowl, dumped Count Chocula to the top edge and poured milk on it. Since no one was around, I settled in front of the TV to eat as I watched a news show. Nothing else was on this time of the day.

At the top of the hour, I flipped the channel to

Captain Kangaroo. Even though it was a little kid show, Mr. Bunny Rabbit and Mr. Moose were so silly, it was hard not to laugh.

As the final notes of the theme song played, I went upstairs and put on Mom's corduroy bell-bottoms and a turtleneck. The wind rattled the panes of glass, and cold seeped through the window frames in my room.

"Ally, come here once," Grandma called. "Do you want to work on a project?"

With nothing else on the agenda, I nodded yes. Grandma directed me to the living room to get the plastic bag filled with crocheted granny squares. We were going to piece together an afghan.

Dumping the squares onto the carpet, I sorted through the various colors. My job was to lay them out in a pattern so that Grandma could stitch them together. Each square was made with different colors of scrap yarn for the inner part. The outer edges were all the same shade of olive green. People in the '70s just couldn't get enough of that color.

The pattern called for twelve squares across and thirty up and down. Puzzling over the layout, I moved squares from spot to spot, doing my best to duplicate the pattern of the afghan I remembered from home. Now I know where that came from. Satisfied with the final product, I took the six leftover squares and put them together for the matching pillow.

Approving the final product, Grandma picked up the squares in order so she could start stitching them together. That would take a couple of days. I looked forward to having something from my previous life that I could physically hang onto in this life.

The rest of the day was spent reading, listening to records and writing in Mom's diary. My resolution to record each day's events hadn't gone too well, so I had catching up to do.

I relished every moment away from school. Watching the news that night, the low-pressure system sat squarely over our state. Looked like we were in for another snow day. No stomach aches tonight!

Chapter 44

It was shaping up to be a decent week. Or, as good as any week could be living someone else's life. School was canceled again the next day. Hearing the big snowplows on our street, I knew it'd be our last day off for this storm system.

By noon the wind had died down, and the sun peeked from behind the clouds. After numerous phone calls, Vicky, Connie, Tammy, Theresa and I decided to meet at St. Joseph's parking lot to play on the massive hill left behind by the plows.

We weren't the only ones who wanted to play *King of the Hill.* A dozen kids swarmed the mounds of snow by the time we got there. As the oldest ones there, us girls conquered that hill, taking no prisoners.

Cheeks bright red from the cold, we persistently chased the younger kids off the mountain. As the sun sank into the horizon, we abandoned our positions and ran to the convent to say hello to the sisters.

The smell of freshly baked cookies wafted from the kitchen to the front entryway as Sister Joan tugged the door open.

"Good afternoon, girls," she said cheerily.

"Good afternoon, Sister," we replied together.

"Come on in."

Stamping snow from our boots, the five of us

stepped into the convent.

“Looks like you could use some warming up. May I interest you in some hot chocolate and chocolate chip cookies?

The gleam in our eyes was all the confirmation that she needed. “Take a seat. I’ll be right back.”

Once again, I was surprised by the sisters. They were so down to earth and nice, nothing like the ones depicted in old movies: tyrants who ran their classrooms with an iron fist, a wooden ruler ever at hand, waiting to rap the knuckles of unruly students.

After we enjoyed our snack and visiting with our teachers, we set off for home. On the way back, we made plans to meet at the high school the next night for the basketball game.

As if the week wasn’t already going well enough, Richard missed school Friday because he was sick. I couldn’t believe my good fortune.

With the weekend approaching, everyone had ants in their pants, waiting for school to get out. I could have stayed there all night. It was such a relief not to have to put up with Richard for a day.

If only he could miss the rest of the year or however long I was grounded here. Not that I wanted him to die, but maybe if he got something really bad, they’d hold him back a year. I’d heard that was a thing back in the day. If he repeated seventh grade, then he’d be out of Mom’s hair when she resumed her life, so it’d be a win for both of us.

I doubted that I could be that lucky, but it was enjoyable to think about.

After school, I ran upstairs to get ready for the game. Wanting to look my best, I put on Mom's new blue jeans, the button-down flannel shirt I'd bought on clearance at J.C. Penney after Christmas, and the silver bracelet engraved with Mom's name.

After gobbling down my fish sticks and Tater Tots, I brushed my teeth, put on the peach Avon lip gloss and dabbed a little Love's Baby Soft inside each elbow, on my wrists and behind each ear lobe.

Glancing in the mirror, I gave myself a nod of approval. The shag had finally grown out long enough that I could pin my hair back and the cut didn't look quite so atrocious, my wardrobe was evolving, and getting by without the glasses whenever I could, I appeared considerably less geeky than I had four months ago.

Noticing Grandma lost in thought at the dining room table, I stepped into the back closet, grabbed my ski jacket and swapped out the moon boots for tennies.

As Vicky came up the walk, I yelled goodbye to Grandma and rushed out the front door. I knew she wouldn't approve of how I was dressed. But, even if it was below zero, I wouldn't be caught dead walking into the high school wearing dorky boots, a stocking cap and fuzzy mittens.

As Vicky and I trekked to the school, I kept my hands in my pockets and stepped around the icy spots on the sidewalk. Vicky wore mittens but, other than that, she wasn't dressed much warmer than I was.

We entered the toasty school, and a sigh escaped

my lips. With the gym doors open, warm air, blasting music, and cheering voices greeted us. The players ran drills, the band blared "Rockin' Robin," kids bounced to the rhythm in the stands, and the cheerleaders danced along both sides of the court.

"Twenty-five cents," said a woman seated behind a table just inside the doors.

Jarred from my trance, I stuffed my hand into my jeans pocket and dug for the quarter with fingers I could hardly feel. Handing the money to the lady, an X was marked on the back of my hand with a magic marker. Once Vicky was in, we searched for our group of friends.

It was a back and forth game, but none of us girls really watched much of it. Our eyes were fixed on the visiting-team players. I knew the team now as the Eagles, but back then, they were the Indians. Apparently, that was an acceptable mascot in the '70s. Technically, the guys were Indians, as in American Indians. Their high school was located on the reservation north of town. Dark skin, jet-black hair, all muscles. They looked pretty fine.

Our team pulled it off in the end, winning by one point. The whole gym erupted into applause and cheers, and the students spilled onto the floor and surrounded the team as the opposing players shuffled off to the away-team locker room.

Energized by the festive mood, everyone wanted to keep the celebration going. Most of the high schoolers headed to parties or Union Lunch. Junior high kids were relegated to Sandy's because there were only so many booths at Union Lunch, and the older kids got first dibs.

Robert had just started working the register at Sandy's restaurant after his birthday. If he rung up my order, maybe he'd be cool like last time and throw in a couple extra fries or burgers on my tray for free. As annoying as older brothers can be, I was starting to see that both he and Howard had their good points. They could actually be nice to me when they put their minds to it.

Maneuvering my way through the tangle of kids, I took a spot in Robert's line while the other girls secured a table.

They were chatting and laughing in the corner booth when I approached with the stacked tray. Thanks to Robert, I doled out an abundance of burgers, fries and soda to everyone.

Even though Sandy's always served their fries hot and salty, Patty ripped open two little salt packets to sprinkle over hers.

"Yikes, that's a lot of salt. How can you eat something so salty?" I asked.

"Easy," she replied. "You add enough ketchup to balance it out." She proceeded to rip open four little packs of ketchup.

"There you go," I said.

We had fun talking about the game as we ate. Before we knew it, the time was approaching ten o'clock, Vicky's curfew. Because it was cold, her dad said he would bring her, Gina and me home. He told Vicky to call when we were ready.

At five to ten, the three of us said our goodbyes, left the warm restaurant and walked a block to the nearest payphone. Vicky dropped a dime in the pay slot, turned the rotary dial five times and got her dad on the phone. She told him we were ready to be picked up and would wait for him by the phone booth.

Fifteen minutes went by, then twenty, then twenty-five and still no sign of her dad. By this time, it was bitterly cold. The wind slapped at our cheeks, and the three of us crowded next to the phone stand in an attempt to generate some heat. *Where is an actual phone booth when you need one*? This thing wasn't doing diddly-squat to keep us warm.

"Maybe we should call him again," Gina said, her voice shaking as her teeth rattled against each other.

"Does anyone have another dime?" Vicky gave us a worried glance. "That was my last one."

Gina and I both shook our heads. Chilled to the bone, I regretted my decision to leave the moon boots, stocking hat and mittens at home. Even with my hands in my pockets and hopping up and down like crazy, I still couldn't get warm. "We sh-should head back to Sandy's," I said.

"But what about when Dad gets here? He won't know where to find us," Vicky replied. We were in a pickle, no doubt about it. After a brief discussion, we decided to wait it out. Finally, twenty minutes later, Vicky's dad pulled up in his work vehicle.

Vicky, Gina and I raced to the van and piled onto the middle bench seat. The heat blowing from the front of the vehicle burned our faces. None of us could talk the first couple of blocks because we were so cold. When Vicky could finally get something out, she let loose on her dad.

"What the heck, Dad! Where were you?"

Mr. Holtz glanced at her in the rearview mirror. "We were just throwing a pizza in the oven when you called. I figured I'd eat quick before I came and got you."

"Oh my God, seriously, Dad? Did you look at the temperature tonight? It's freezing!"

He turned and glanced at Vicky, his brown eyes showing concern.

"You knew we were by the payphone waiting for you. I can't believe you ate a stupid pizza while we were freezing to death."

"I guess I didn't realize it was that cold."

"I cannot wait until I get my license, and I won't have to depend on you anymore." With that, Vicky crossed her arms over her chest and slammed her mouth shut. This was another one of those times when I wanted to tell her to give her dad some slack. She'd miss him when he was gone.

When I got home, I couldn't wait to get inside. Thanking Mr. Holtz for the ride, I flung open the side door, jumped out and raced up the back steps. Discarded jacket and shoes leaving a trail behind me, I grabbed the granny square afghan, ran upstairs, and said goodnight to Grandma. Without even changing my clothes, I wrapped the afghan around me, crawled into bed and covered myself head to toe with the sheet and blankets.

My teeth chattered so hard my jaw hurt. I'd never been so cold in my entire life. I rocked back and forth, trying to generate heat. It took fifteen minutes to fall asleep, and when I finally did, I dreamt about being deserted in the woods on a cold winter day.

The next morning, I woke up with a sore throat and a throbbing head. It took considerable effort to crawl out of bed and untangle myself from the afghan.

Grabbing clean clothes, I made my way downstairs to take a shower. As I undressed, I noticed that Mom's engraved bracelet was missing from my wrist. In a panic, I ran back to my bedroom, tore apart the bedding, and searched frantically between the sheets. No luck there, I retraced my path from the night before and scoured every square inch of the house.

Defeated, I locked myself in the bathroom, slid to the floor and broke into tears. With all the places we'd been Friday and all the snow on the ground, there was no way I'd ever find Mom's bracelet again.

I felt horrible. That bracelet was probably so special to her, and now I had to go and lose it. *Could this life suck any worse?*

Chapter 45

What was that expression? Don't ask a question if you're not prepared to hear the answer.

Yes, in fact, Mom's life could suck worse.

Even with the nasty cold, no amount of begging would get Grandma to let me stay home sick Monday. So, there I was bright and early Monday morning shuffling through the snow, bundled up like an Eskimo chilling at the North Pole.

One thing at school actually made the trip worthwhile. We got a new classmate. Bobbi Jo's cousin Denise Cook had enrolled at St. Joseph's. She was temporarily living with the Howells on their farm. That meant one more girl in our group. There was strength in numbers. Or something like that.

The second week Denise was in school, she pulled me, Vicky and Tammy aside at the end of the day as everyone was packing their bookbags.

"Did you know that Bobbi Jo's birthday is Friday?"

"No, I didn't," I said. I didn't actually know when anybody's birthdays were.

"Yah," said Denise, "My aunt and uncle aren't doing anything to celebrate because they're driving across state to visit their new grandkid."

"I didn't know Bobbi Jo was an aunt again," said Vicky, a smile breaking out on her face.

"Yup. But don't say anything to her right now

because it's bugging her that her parents care more about the new baby than her."

"Wow, that stinks," said Tammy. "We should do something to celebrate Bobbi Jo's birthday at school."

"That'd be really cool," said Denise. "Well, gotta catch the bus."

"Bye," we said in unison.

Vicky, Tammy and I discussed the situation and decided to chip in and get Bobbi Jo a gift from the drugstore after Home Ec. on Wednesday. We could make cupcakes for the class at my house.

Friday morning, Sister Martha gave us permission to hand out the cupcakes after prayers. The gifts and snacks were on the stage. When the last prayer was said, I stepped onto the stage and pulled the velvet curtain aside. Tammy reached for the Tupperware container with the cupcakes, and Vicky scooped up the gifts. It was my job to make the announcement.

"Hey, everybody. We just want to wish Bobbi Jo a happy birthday and congratulate her on becoming an aunt again."

Sister Martha started a round of applause and broke into the happy birthday song. When it was over, she had Bobbi Jo stand up to say a couple of words.

Bobbi Jo had the Cheshire Cat look on her face, not exactly the reaction I'd anticipated. "Thanks, everyone. That was really cool of you to think of me for my birthday even though it's kind of early. My birthday's April 7, not February 7."

Vicky, Tammy and I turned three different shades

of red. Denise just about fell out of her desk as she tried to hold her laughter in.

Richard glanced at the three of us and rolled his eyes. "What a bunch of nerds."

"And another thing, none of my sisters had any kids lately, so I'm not an aunt again," added Bobbi Jo brightly.

Denise and Bobbi Jo are in cahoots! My state fluctuated between embarrassment and complete annoyance. *How could they do that to us?*

Sister Martha held the empty piece of Tupperware. I slunk up to the podium to retrieve it. Yanking open my desk, I shoved the container inside and slammed the wood top shut.

At that point, everyone in the class, other than me, Tammy and Vicky, was laughing. Even Sister Martha joined in. I slumped further down in my seat. Now Richard had more ammunition to make fun of me. And things were only going to get worse.

I had an appointment with Dr. Ackerman two weeks from Monday to discuss putting braces on my teeth. *It wasn't fair. I'd gone through that torture two years ago.* Mom can deal with it this time. *Any day now, you can jump back into your own stupid life, Mom.*

At least I had Valentine's Day to look forward to before then. I'd always liked exchanging valentines, and it was Howard's birthday too.

Vicky and I made a trip to the drugstore to buy Valentines. The best ones I could find were this cartoon character called Holly Hobbie. The pack came with thirty cards, but that wasn't quite enough because we now had thirty-six kids in our class.

I had no intention of giving Richard a valentine, so taking him and me off, that left thirty-four kids. Full-sized Valentine cards near the checkout cost ten cents each, so, rather than getting a whole other pack, I'd get four of those for Mom's closest friends.

Thursday night, I spent an hour sorting through the cards to choose the ideal one for each classmate. I didn't want to give any mushy cards to the boys and give them the wrong impression. Those were saved for the girls as a joke.

In art class, we'd decorated shoeboxes with hearts and glitter to make Valentine mailboxes. On Valentine's Day, the boxes were placed on our desks. Sister Cecilia played the record "Dominique" as we made our way through the aisles sorting through our cards to get the right ones to drop into each box. Kids who brought treats from home distributed them at the same time.

Sister made us go through our homework from the night before and do a Valentine's Wordsearch before we could eat the snacks. To avoid any hard feelings, as some kids got more valentines than other kids, we weren't allowed to open the boxes until school was dismissed.

I didn't mind waiting to check out the cards at home, but I couldn't wait to eat the snacks. The frosting on the cupcakes smelled so good; it was hard to resist taking a nibble.

All in all, it was a fun day. Richard was somewhat less obnoxious than usual. I shoved the Valentine box into my clear plastic book bag and walked home on my own because Vicky and Tammy had to help their siblings get their Valentine boxes home.

Ten seconds after entering the house, I dumped the contents of the shoebox onto the kitchen table. There was a good number of cards and some candy too. Kids gave either one or the other, except for Stacey, who'd taped a sucker onto the back of each of her valentines. Maybe this was her way of drumming up more business for her dad, Dr. Ackerman.

One at a time, I picked up each Valentine, looked at the picture and then turned it over to see who it was from. Seeing one card flipped the opposite way, I read the writing on the back first.

"To Allison from Richard," was written in neat, small cursive. It wasn't Richard's crappy penmanship. His sister must've written them out for him. Turning it over, I saw a picture of a dog. The card said, "Doggonit, Won't You Be My Valentine?"

The Valentine, designed to be funny, brought tears to my eyes. *Can't you be nice one freakin' day of the year?*

The excitement gone, I shoved all the Valentines back in the box. Grandma would probably want to see them later, but I felt like throwing all of them in the garbage.

Chapter 46

Luckily, the day wouldn't be a complete bust. On the counter sat a frosted banana-nut cake with sixteen candles sticking out from it. That was pretty nice of Grandma to make Howard's favorite cake from scratch, considering how much she hated bananas. She'd probably been gagging when she was mixing the batter.

While fish sticks were the normal Friday fare, since it was Howard's birthday and it wasn't Lent yet, he got to choose the dinner menu. Meatloaf, baked potatoes and canned green beans awaited us. The gift opening came first, so Grandpa could watch before he went to work.

Howard received a couple of albums, an artist sketch pad and the game *Risk*. We didn't even have to play it for me to know that it would start arguments. That's how all board games worked in this family.

For his gift, Robert got a Moody Blues album. He played it immediately because "Nights in White Satin" — or what he called the perfect prom song — was on side A.

Grandma gave me a hand-sewn skirt. She called it a maxi. Probably because it was the opposite of a miniskirt. The red-and-white houndstooth fabric fell all the way to my toes. It seemed to be the hottest fashion lately. *Yay, Mom. You're on the front edge of a trend for once.*

Unbelievably, the boys and I made it through the inaugural game of *Risk* without any raised voices or Robert flipping the board. As per usual, brainiac Howard won.

Saturday, Vicky and I strolled downtown to Robinson's Jewelry. Mom was one of the few girls in her class who didn't have her ears pierced, and I intended to do something about it.

The plan was to pick out a pair of pierced earrings and have Grandma wait on me. I'd been saving Mom's allowance to buy them. Even if Grandma objected, she wouldn't yell at me in front of Vicky. Besides, I was a paying customer.

We entered the store, and Grandma glanced up from a display case, her head tilted as she greeted us.

"Hi, girls," she said. "Can I help you with something?"

"I'm here to pick out a pair of pierced earrings," I said authoritatively.

Grandma gave me a skeptical look but unlocked the spinning display case nonetheless. Turning the display every so often, Vicky and I pulled out various earrings, holding them up to our earlobes and checking our reflections in the mirror.

The selection was limited, but I finally found a pair of pewter turtles that caught my eye. Not sure how Mom felt about turtles, but I thought they were cute. Turning the cardboard over, I realized that they were out of my price range.

Shoot. I bit my lip as I considered starting the search again.

Seeing my dilemma, Mr. Robinson, the owner, stepped forward and told me I could put money down on the pair that I wanted and put them on layaway. He said if I stopped in every week and put more money towards the purchase, they'd be mine in a month or so.

Credit for kids? That worked for me. With my consent, Mr. Robinson slipped into the backroom to put the earrings in the layaway area.

Hands on her hips, Grandma addressed me in a low voice. "Ally, didn't I say you needed to be in high school to have your ears pierced?"

Maybe. But I was in it to win it now. "Every girl in my class has pierced ears," I said, pointing to Vicky's earlobes as proof.

"If every girl in your class jumped off a cliff, would you want to do that too?" Parents have used that line since the beginning of time. I wasn't deterred.

"It's not like getting my ears pierced is dangerous."

"I understand that, but once they're pierced, there's no going back," said Grandma, in what she probably thought was a reasonable voice. "Why don't you take a look at the clip-on earrings? We've got a nice selection. I've been wearing them for years."

"Only old ladies wear clip-on earrings!"

Grandma ignored the remark and continued. "Well, even if you can come up with the rest of the money, how are you going to get your ears pierced?"

"Got it all figured out. Theresa's mom is a nurse, and she can pierce my ears at their house. She did it for Connie and Theresa and a couple other girls in our class."

Grandma's stance softened. "Sounds like you've put some thought into this. But you're obligated to come up with the rest of the money. No begging Dad."

Bouncing on my toes, I did my best to contain my excitement. "I can stop by every week when I get my allowance. Plus, I'll take on some extra babysitting jobs until I have enough to cover the rest." I grabbed Vicky's elbow. "Bye!"

"Bye, Ally. Bye, Vicky," said Grandma as she shut the drawer of the cash register, shaking her head and smiling.

By Monday, the excitement of the earring purchase had faded, and I dragged my feet on the trip over to the dentist's office after school.

After I was seated in the dentist's chair, Dr. Ackerman poked around in my mouth.

"Yup," he said. "Time to get all those little doggies back in line."

He thought he was funny. I didn't appreciate his sense of humor. After almost gagging during the impressions, the appointment was set for me to come in a week to get the braces on.

I still remember how sore my teeth felt when I'd gotten my braces on at the orthodontist's office when I was in fifth grade. That was nothing compared to the torture that Dr. Ackerman put me through a few days later.

Mom's teeth were not only crooked but crowded together too. Instead of gluing brackets to my teeth like the orthodontist did, Dr. Ackerman forcibly shoved a metal bracket around each tooth. The icing on the cake was inserting what felt like barbed wire into each of the brackets to pull them all together. The wire was just long enough that it poked the back inside of my mouth on both sides.

That night all I could eat for dinner was applesauce with crushed aspirin for garnish.

The pain intensified the next morning when I got to school.

"Didn't know dogs got braces," Richard said, pointing at me and snorting. "Must be 'ruff' being a brace face." The boys around him dutifully joined in the laughter.

There wasn't much I could do except count down the weeks until the miserable things came off. For the time being, I'd have to get used to them and stay as far from Richard as possible. The pain from the braces would wear off. Who knew if the pain from his words ever would.

Chapter 47

With a decent amount of snow still on the ground, Vicky and I planned a trip to Pine Hill the first Saturday in March. We'd gotten annual ski patches at the beginning of the season and were determined to get as much use out of them as we could.

The first time we'd gone there in January, the scene I saw before me from the top step of the school bus was strange. No chair lifts, just two tow ropes powered by ancient tractors. That rope chewed through ski mittens like nobody's business. The old A-frame chalet must have been around for at least fifty years. No indoor toilets. A trip to the outhouse meant freezing your rear end off.

We'd been to the hill a half-dozen times since then. Vicky had skied since she was little, so she did the harder runs the first time out. The transition from snowboard to skis took me a bit, but now I was comfortable on the blue square, Pine Hill's most-challenging run.

It was hilarious the first time I did that run. Vicky went ahead of me so she could wait at the bottom of the hill to make sure that I got down safely. Once she was positioned there, I took off, reveling in the wind going through my hair, something I hadn't experienced before since I'd always worn a helmet. I kept Vicky in sight as I slalomed down the hill.

The closer I got, the bigger her eyes widened. Her thick glass lenses magnified her pupils. Taking a quick left at the bottom of the hill, I sprayed her with a shower of snow. The expression on her face was priceless.

"Holy cow! Did those new skis you got for Christmas come with lessons?"

"No," I said, holding my laughter in, "Guess I'm just more confident with these than the rental skis I used last year."

"I guess," Vicky replied, shaking her head in amazement.

Ever since that day, Vicky and I had skied together on the same runs. This morning we got a ride to the hill from Mr. Holtz, who had a carpet delivery in the area. We unloaded our skis and boots from his paneled van, scurried over to the bench by the chalet to get our gear on and then hit the slopes. We skied all morning, relishing in the fresh air and the sun beating on our cheeks.

"You look like you're getting sunburned," said Vicky.

"Really?" I took off my mitten and felt my cheek with the back of my hand. "You may be right. Who'd think a person could get sunburned in the middle of winter? Maybe we should take a break and get lunch."

Vicky was on the same page. We skied over to the chalet, unlatched our ski boots, then laid our skis against the wooden ski holder before clumping into the chalet.

The muggy building was packed with kids. For fifty cents, we got a Sloppy Joe, a small bag of plain potato chips and a cup of hot chocolate. After eating,

Vicky suggested we stay out of the sun for a bit and go to the top of the hill and ski on the cross-country trail that wound through the woods.

This was my first time on the trail. The view was pretty. And it was so serene. We had the snowy landscape and quiet woods to ourselves. Forty-five minutes into the trek, probably a quarter-mile from the chalet, Vicky caught her ski tip on a tree root and fell to the ground. Her knee twisted as she lurched forward.

Moving as fast as I could, I unbuckled from my skis and stumbled to her side, reaching out to help her get to her feet. She waved my hand away. "I can't get up," she said, wincing in pain.

"Would it be better if you took your skis off?" I asked.

Vicky shrugged.

As gently as I could, I disengaged her boots from the skis. Every time I brushed her right leg, she let out a yelp. "Are you going to be able to stand if I help you?"

"I don't think I can get up. It hurts too much." Tears glistened on her eyelashes.

"What do you want me to do?"

"Go back to the chalet. Find a guy with a red vest. They're supposed to help people."

The last segment of the trail was uphill. It'd be a lot easier with cross-country skis. "Should I walk back or ski?"

"I don't care what you do, just get going," Vicky replied crabbily.

"Fine." I jammed my ski boots back into the bindings. It took a good fifteen minutes to work my way back to the chalet and then another five to find one of the helper guys.

He grabbed another guy, and they took off toward the cross-country path, dragging an orange sled behind them.

Taking a vacant seat on the bench outside the chalet, I waited for Vicky to be brought back. Twenty minutes later, I spied the two guys pulling her on the sled. By this time, the sky was varying shades of pink and orange. Parents were pulling into the parking lot to get their kids. Seeing Mr. Holtz parking the family station wagon, I flagged him down. When he saw Vicky on the sled, he bolted from the car, not even bothering to shut the door.

Chapter 48

Fortunately, it turned out to be just a sprain, so Vicky only had to wear a brace on her leg for two weeks. She wasn't able to go to the snowmobile races at the county fairgrounds, which was kind of a big deal back then, so I ended up going with Tammy and Sharon. Vicky probably wouldn't have gone anyhow. For some reason, ever since the skiing incident, she'd been miffed with me.

Even though all the spectators smelled like gasoline after spending a day so close to the snowmobile track, the three of us had fun. Some of the guys flew around the track so fast they spun out and crashed into the bales of hay lining the perimeter.

Between a couple of the big races, little kids raced miniature snowmobiles. Full out, the Kitty Kats went maybe ten miles an hour. The big sleds could go more than fifty miles an hour.

At intermission, we bought snacks from the concession stand. In support of Tammy and Sharon, who'd given up candy for Lent, I got popcorn instead of a candy bar.

As unbelievable as it seemed, I'd been living Mom's life for seven months now. Some days, it seemed so real to me that I almost forgot I had another life. Every time a major event or holiday rolled around, I was sure that I'd wake up the next day and everything would be back to normal.

But, so far, that hadn't happened. I guess the adage, "You can get used to just about anything," was true. While the Richard situation completely stressed me out, and my stomach still hurt terribly on school nights, I was learning to live with it. For the life of me, I couldn't understand what triggered this. Truthfully, he picked on all the not-cool kids, but he really had it out for Mom for some reason.

Other than Richard, I liked the rest of the kids in Mom's class. Or tolerated them in the case of Laura. It seemed like I was building actual friendships with everyone else, though.

Were there lessons I had to learn before God would give me my life back? *Did I have to become a better person to earn my way back?* It was a thought at the top of my mind most days.

Lent was going well. Last year I'd tried giving up yelling at Brock and Brayden. Didn't even make it a week. This year I decided to give up my real life — which I'd come to realize was way better than I had ever thought it was — and continue to live Mom's for another forty days. Every morning my commitment was renewed, whether I wanted it to be or not.

One good thing about Lent was that we got out of school early on Thursdays. Stations of the Cross started at two o'clock, and we were dismissed forty-five minutes later when they were done. That meant twenty-five minutes less dealing with Richard and first dibs on the snacks and TV set when I got home from school.

Each week kids from one grade got to do the

readings for each station. Sister Cecilia picked me to be one of the readers when our class was in charge. I practiced reading Station Twelve out loud four times to Grandma the night before to make sure that I didn't mess it up.

By the time the third weekend in March arrived, Vicky had her knee brace off and was able to go with the rest of our troop to Girl Scout winter camp.

I rode to Camp Red Rocks in Mrs. Caruso's woody station wagon with five other girls. Monica and Vicky shared the front bench seat with Mrs. Caruso, and the rest of us squeezed onto the middle seat. The back of the vehicle was loaded with food, toilet paper, cooking supplies, paper plates and plastic silverware, plus our gear.

We left directly from school Friday. Our suitcases and pillows had been piled at the bottom of the staircase leading to our classroom. Looking over what everyone else brought, I'd stomped my foot. *Dang it. Forgot my pillow.*

I scurried to the library and asked Sister Margaret Mary if I could use the phone to call Grandma. The phone was picked up after just two rings.

"Connors, Marilyn speaking."

"Mom, it's Ally." *Like she wouldn't recognize the voice.* "I forgot my pillow for the camping trip. Can you bring it to school today before we leave?"

"Ally, you had a packing list. If you didn't bring it, that's your responsibility, not mine."

"I totally get that, but we have to sleep on the floor all weekend. How am I supposed to sleep with no pillow?"

"Maybe someone will bring an extra one. Either way, you'll survive."

I ground my teeth. "Fine," I growled. "See you Sunday."

"Have fun."

Whatever... "I'll try. Bye."

Our group was the first to arrive at camp. Grabbing everything we could carry, we spilled out of the car and trudged into the log cabin. It was freezing inside. Each scout was instructed to go to the stockpile outside and bring in an armful of logs.

Everyone had earned their Fire-Starting badges, so allegedly any one of us could've started the fire, but Vicky got the nod since they had a wood fireplace at their house.

With torn up newspapers as tinder, the fire sputtered to life in seconds. Just as quickly, smoke billowed out of the fireplace and into the cabin. Guess they never learned about chimney flues when they earned that dumb badge.

Vicky scrambled to turn the flue, so the smoke vented up the chimney like it was supposed to. The rest of us yanked open windows to clear the air in the lodge before the other girls arrived.

By four o'clock, everyone was there. We were divided into groups for dinner duty: food prep, table setting, table clearing, dishes.

No meat on Fridays, so the menu consisted of tuna fish sandwiches, corn, potato chips and Hawaiian Punch. Mrs. Ledoux sent up two pans of chocolate butterscotch squares for dessert, making me glad once again that I hadn't given up sweets for Lent.

Rhonda Gilbert and I got the easy job of setting tables. Even with the inexperienced chefs, dinner was really good. It'd be pretty hard to mess up that simple meal.

As the clean-up crew worked, the rest of us sorted through paper, pens and markers for a badge we'd be working on. To earn the Reader badge, we were required to make a children's book. We'd write the story together, and each girl would illustrate one page. When the pages were complete, the book would be stapled together and donated to St. Joseph's library.

Thanks to some decent artists in the troop, the book turned out well. It'd be fun to see what the little kids at school thought about it.

The next item on the agenda was learning a dance for World Girl Scout Day. Each Girl Scout troop in town was tasked with performing a traditional dance from a different country. We were assigned Israel and worked on learning The Hora.

As the song played, the tempo continually increased. By the time we'd finished running through it four times, everyone was out of breath, our cheeks pink from exertion — that and the heat emanating from the blazing fire.

Wouldn't be Girl Scout camp without camp songs. We sang "Barges," "Kookaburra," "An Austrian Went Yodeling," "Baby Bumble Bee," "Swimming Hole," "Down by the Bay," "I Love to Go a Wandering," and "Waddley-acha," which got us all laughing as we tried to keep up with the hand motions that got faster as the song went along.

At the leaders' request, we positioned ourselves in new seats apart from our friends. We ended the night holding hands singing "Make New Friends." Bonding as it was, everyone scurried back to their buddies as soon as the last word was sung.

When everyone had their spots staked out for their blankets or sleeping bags, I asked around to see if anyone had an extra pillow. Striking out, I resorted to wadding up my ski jacket and stuffing it under my head for a makeshift pillow.

It took almost an hour for the chatter to subside. After several threats by the leaders, it was finally quiet, and the girls fell asleep. For once, my stomach wasn't hurting, but I couldn't get comfortable without a real pillow. After an hour of tossing and turning, I became aware of Vicky's slow and steady breathing. Stealthily, I lifted her head, slid her pillow out from under it, and slid my jacket back in its place.

After that, I slept soundly the rest of the night. Vicky couldn't say the same. She was not a happy camper when she woke up the next morning with a crick in her neck. What had seemed like a sound idea at the time turned out to be a bust. She was ticked.

Our troop had a full day planned. First, we made a breakfast of scrambled eggs, bacon and toast. Mmm… bacon. That's a good start.

After breakfast, we worked on the Animal Kingdom badge by hiking in the woods to search for birds. Stacey and Laura brought cameras from home, so they worked on their Photography badge at the same time.

As cold as it was, we saw a surprising amount of birds. After a while, one bird looked pretty much like the next to me, and my feet were freezing. I was more than ready to go back to the cabin. Fortunately, I was on chef's duty for lunch, so I got to bug out early to cut up fruit for a salad.

The big activity for the day was cross-country skiing. The lean-to had numerous sets of skis, boots and poles. As there wasn't enough equipment for everyone to go out at once, we broke into two groups.

It took a good twenty minutes for everyone in the first group to dig through the gear to find our proper sizes. That done, Mrs. Ackerman led the way as we entered the woods. We glided along a mile-long path around the edge of the camp. The route had been worn down by other groups of scouts who'd been camping there earlier in the winter.

At one point, we had to go through a ditch. We were supposed to go down slowly and use our poles to push ourselves up the other side. Somehow, I managed to get the back end of my ski on one side of the ditch and the front end on the other, and when I put my weight down, the ski snapped in two.

Everyone heard the noise. Mrs. Ackerman made her way back to where I was stuck and helped me get my skis off.

"That's the end of that," she said matter-of-factly. "You'll have to walk back. Mrs. Caruso, can you finish the route?"

Mrs. Caruso took the lead position and set off with the rest of the girls. I felt terrible. Not only had I broken the ski, but I didn't get to finish the course, so I may have ruined Mom's chance to earn the badge.

I trudged back to the cabin, trying to balance the skis in my arms and keep up with Mrs. Ackerman, who was still on her skis. Dumping what was left of the skis in the lean-to, I slunk back into the main building and stoked the fire. Hopefully, there'd be enough skis for all the girls in the next group to go out. I didn't want to mess up anyone else's shot at getting the badge.

Vicky hadn't gone out skiing because she didn't want to risk hurting her knee again. She didn't say a word when she saw me. That pillow thing was coming back to bite me.

That night we took a hike in the frigid nighttime air to identify the stars in the late-winter sky. With Vicky still giving me the cold shoulder, when we got back, I staked out a place to sleep next to Patty. Even with just a jacket for a pillow, the fresh air wore me out, and I drifted off to sleep in a fraction of the time that it had taken the night before.

We had to be back to St. Joseph's for Mass by ten o'clock Sunday morning, so our breakfast was a simple one. Bandana-clad heads nodded during Mass that day. At least we had Father Dom's peppy guitar playing to help keep us awake.

Chapter 49

Easter came and went, and I was still living Mom's life. April finally arrived with its longer days and somewhat warmer weather, making everyone itch for spring. On a bright Saturday afternoon, with temperatures in the mid-forties, girls from Mom's Ponytail Softball league met at the technical school parking lot for a pickup game of softball.

With no school on the weekends, we had the whole lot to ourselves. Vicky brought carpet sample squares to use as bases, Gina had a softball, Patty provided a wooden bat, and we each had our own ball gloves.

We did eeny, meenie, miny, mo to pick captains. With only five girls per side, the batting team had to provide the catcher. Any balls hit to right field were foul.

The running kept us all warm enough. Drawing fresh spring air into my lungs invigorated me. After four innings, our team was down five to four. The sun dipped behind a bank of clouds, and it was getting chilly, so we called the game.

Before we left, we checked out the humongous snow pile where all the snow had been stacked throughout the winter, and each took a guess as to what day the snow would be completely melted. Since Monica lived nearby, it was her job to keep an eye on the hill and report back to the rest of us.

School was in the fourth quarter, so the eighth

graders were turning over some of their duties to the seventh-graders, including washing dishes for the priests. It was an after-school commitment. Only kids who didn't ride the bus were allowed to help.

A different group of three boys or three girls covered each weeknight. The job wasn't too bad because sometimes Father Dom was there, and he'd joke around with his helpers or hand out snacks.

Vicky was still mad at me, so she formed her own group with Theresa and Patty. Tammy, Connie and I teamed up to work Friday afternoons.

My favorite job was rinsing the dishes. The rectory sink had a hand sprayer, which was good for rinsing dishes and instigating water fights. Regardless of how much water got splashed around, we always made sure the kitchen was spic and span by the time we left.

One day when we got there and stacked dishes in the soapy water, Connie shrieked and pointed toward the sink. A gargantuan spider hid between two plates. That caused me and Tammy to scream too.

Father Dom ran in from his office. "What's the matter?" The three of us pointed at the stack of plates from a safe distance.

Stepping toward the sink, Father reached his hand in and grabbed the spider by one leg, resulting in more screams. A smile burst out on his face, and he laughed.

"Don't you girls know a fake spider when you see one?"

"What?" I said.

"Are you kidding?" Tammy exclaimed.

He stepped forward with the spider in his hand so we could see it closer. Sure enough, it was made of black rubber and had beady red plastic eyes.

"Who put that there?" Connie asked.

"It wasn't me," said Father. "I'm going to guess it was the boys."

"Keith, Greg and Kurt were here last night," said Connie. "I wonder if it was them?"

"Those creeps," I said. "They're just as bad as my brothers."

"We have to get them back," Tammy said, a devious glint in her eyes. "And I've got the perfect plan."

"I'm going to pretend I didn't hear that," said Father Dom as he headed back to his office. "Just don't do anything I wouldn't do."

"We won't, Father," we said in unison.

The plan was put in place for the following Thursday afternoon. At the end of the school day, Tammy and I volunteered to clean the chalkboard erasers outside. As soon as we got to the first floor, we sprinted out the door, ran to the far edge of the football field and snuck in the back door of the rectory. Quietly we made our way to the kitchen, praying that the priests would be far enough away that they couldn't hear us.

Pulling a roll of Scotch tape from the back pocket of Mom's corduroys, I approached the sink. Tammy took the sprayer out of its holder and held the handle down. I rolled tape around the handle several times. Then we placed the sprayer back in its place and quietly went out the side door.

We clapped the abandoned erasers together as we ran back to the school building. We took our time so we could catch our breath. Erasers were returned to the chalkboard ledge with no one any the wiser.

This was too good to miss. When class was dismissed, Tammy, Connie and I hung around the front of the school and waited for Keith, Greg and Kurt to head towards the rectory. We ran to the other side of the school building, and as soon as we saw the boys open the back door of the rectory, we sprinted after them.

Once we got there, we positioned ourselves under the open kitchen window and listened as the boys put down their coats and books and started getting ready to wash the dishes. When we heard someone approach the sink, our three sets of eyeballs popped up over the window sill. We watched as Keith turned the water on full blast.

Water sprayed everywhere. We couldn't have planned it better if we'd tried. Not only did Keith soak his shirt, but Greg and Kurt, who were close behind him, got drenched too. The three of us girls doubled over in laughter.

The next thing we knew, the door flew open, and all three boys came tumbling out. While our instincts told us to run, we were laughing so hard that we couldn't move. Even though the boys were annoyed, before long, they burst out in laughter too.

Thus, began the dish wars. From that point on, all was fair game. The boys tried to retaliate with the same trick, as we figured, but we were careful to check the sprayer handle before we turned on the faucet each week.

In addition to working in the rectory, I was busy with Girl Scouts as the meetings wound down for the year. Plus, I'd signed up to try out for cheerleading.

Personally, I had no burning desire to be a cheerleader, but it was a big deal at St. Joseph's back then. Every girl in Mom's class was trying out for the eighth-grade squad.

Connie's sister Jeanette and another cheerleader from the high school met us in the school basement twice a week after school to teach us the cheers we needed to know for tryouts. After a couple sessions, I was getting into the spirit of things.

While the after-school activities were fun, school was a drag. Grades-wise, I was doing fine, but I still had to contend with Richard harassing me whenever the mood struck him, which, unfortunately, was just about every day.

On top of that, Vicky was still ignoring me after the skiing incident and the camp fiasco. To make things worse, she and Tammy were hanging out now. I was messing everything up for Mom.

Despite the fun times here and there, a black cloud hung over my head. I sulked around school and the house. One cheery note was that we had an early-dismissal day coming up. On Arbor Day, the sixth-, seventh- and eighth-graders from St. Joseph's were excused from school at one o'clock to attend a presentation about trees and the environment at the American Legion.

Classes walked over in groups led by the teachers. Our homeroom was at the tail end. Theresa, Bobbi Jo and I chatted on the way over. When we got there, they took the last two seats in the row of folding chairs, and I started the next row. By chance, Sister Martha directed Vicky to follow me into the same row.

It was awkward sitting there, not saying anything as we waited for the presentation to start. Vicky finally broke the silence with some small talk. A lump rose in my throat. I missed being friends with her. I knew this was just temporary, but I liked having a best friend. In real life, I couldn't really say that I had one.

"Vicky." I struggled with the words, searching for the right thing to say. A sense of remorse ran through me, and words poured out. "I'm so sorry about everything. I should have handled everything better at Pine Hill, and I shouldn't have been such a dope and steal your pillow at camp."

Vicky stared at me for a second and then turned away. "Yah, that wasn't cool," she replied. She sat in silence for a moment and then sighed. "Maybe I overreacted," she continued. "I probably should've just let it go. I know you've been having a hard year."

Tears came to my eyes. It was the first time that anyone in our class acknowledged what had been going on between me and Richard since school started.

"Let's not fight anymore, okay?" asked Vicky.

Afraid my voice would break if I tried to reply, I just nodded.

The two of us continued talking after everyone else left. As we exited the building and walked into the sunshine, the weight of the world lifted from my shoulders. I didn't know if Richard was ever going to stop picking on me, but at least I had Vicky on my side.

Chapter 50

Hard to believe I'd worn braces four months already. Mom's teeth were straightening out so fast. Every time Dr. Ackerman adjusted the wires, my teeth ached for a couple days after, but it was obviously working.

Two more months, and then Dr. Ackerman would make me a retainer. *How can I warn Mom to wear that thing religiously?* She'd thank me if she didn't have to get her teeth redone when she's in her forties.

Cheerleading tryouts were a few weeks away. It was a hot topic for us girls. The guys were even starting to get in on the conversation.

One day after school, as the other kids whipped out of the classroom, I approached Sister Martha to clarify something on our Math assignment.

Bookbag in hand, I started down the back steps. Reaching the landing, I made the turn to go down the next set of steps. Seeing someone on the lower landing, I stopped dead in my tracks, my breath caught in my throat.

Richard lounged against the stair rail. My heart beat so loudly, I could hear it echoing through my skull. *Why isn't he on the bus?* A bad feeling swept over me. I scanned the area to see if anyone else was nearby.

Just him and me. As much as I wanted to retreat

back up the steps and go to the staircase on the far side of the building, I descended the steps, staying close to the wall.

"Halt, dog," he said.

Heat rose to my cheeks. I tried to step around him, but he blocked my path.

"Heard you're trying out for cheerleading."

I kept quiet.

"Dogs can't be cheerleaders," he said, enunciating each word.

I considered him warily, wondering where the conversation was headed, why he was blocking my way, and, for the love of God, why he continued to torture me day after day.

"You sure you wanna try out for cheerleading?"

I remained silent.

"Think anybody'd let a dog join the cheerleading squad?" He stared straight into my eyes. "Nobody wants to hear a puppy yelping on the sidelines."

My jaw dropped open in disbelief.

"As hard as it would be to imagine, if, by some crazy chance you actually make it, I'm dropping out of football and basketball."

My eyebrows furrowed, waiting for him to continue. "I'm not playing any sport if you're on the sideline cheering." That statement caused my eyes to open wide. "Got it?"

Got it? Yes. Care? No. That'd be the best thing ever as far as I was concerned.

With no reaction from me, he went on to clarify his

statement. "I'm the best athlete in this school. If I don't play, St. Joseph's doesn't stand a chance of winning any games. And it'll be all your fault." He paused for effect. "Everyone in this school will hate you."

So that's where this was going. My mind raced to come up with something to say. I didn't want to make Mom's life any worse than it was, but I was so sick of him. The next words out of my mouth surprised even me. "Go ahead and quit. See if I care."

With that, I stepped to the left and hurried past him, turned the corner and headed down the last set of stairs leading to the front entrance of the school.

"You'll regret this, dog!" The words echoed in the empty corridor.

With trembling hands, I pushed through the double doors and sprinted home, tears streaming down my cheeks. Stepping into the house, I dumped my books and shoes by the back door and bolted upstairs. Slamming the bedroom door behind me, I threw myself onto the bed and let the dam break. All the tears I'd stored inside me for the past eight months flooded out at once.

An hour later, Grandma knocked on the door, saying supper was ready. I fibbed and said that I was taking a nap and wouldn't be eating. In reality, I was hungry and thirsty after crying so much, but I didn't want Grandma and the boys to see my swollen eyes. Robert and Howard would probably make fun of me. I just couldn't deal with anything else today.

The rest of the night, I thought through everything

that had gone on since I'd started living Mom's life. How did Mom ever survive this? It wasn't very Christian-like, but I hated Richard for making my life so miserable.

Even though we'd been commanded to love one another the way Jesus loves us, I just couldn't do that. The thought of going to Confession next time made me nauseous. I knew I should confess my terrible thoughts to Father, but I couldn't share the story of this horrible year with anyone.

As soon as it was dark, I pulled down the white window shade and put my nightgown on. I fell into bed, covered my head with the blanket and rocked back and forth as I mulled over what Richard had said.

Should I skip cheerleading tryouts? What would be worse, letting Richard intimidate me from trying out or potentially making eighth grade even more horrible for Mom? What if everyone really did hate her?

I didn't know what to do. Propping up pillows behind me, I tried to get comfortable, but the tightening in my gut caused me to double over in pain.

Chapter 51

The third Friday in May, I woke up after a restless night of sleep with the never-ending residual stomach ache and a throbbing head. Sunbeams crept in around the edges of the shade and fell across the outfit I'd laid out on the dresser.

With a sigh, I got out of bed. After hours of deliberation, I'd made the decision to go to tryouts and let the chips fall where they may. If being a cheerleader was Mom's dream, I wasn't going to give up her one shot because of some bully.

As I brushed my hair in front of the bathroom mirror, I noticed dark circles under my eyes. I splashed cold water on my face and pinched my cheeks, so I didn't look so ghost-like. Makeup would be nice, but all Mom owned was lip gloss.

Wearing Mom's best faded bell-bottom jeans, a short-sleeved blue-striped knit top of hers that was one of my favorites, and the gold cross necklace that she'd received for her First Communion, I poured a bowl of Lucky Charms for breakfast. *Not taking any chances.*

School crawled along for seven hours. When the final bell rang, all of us girls grabbed the bags we'd brought with our clothes for tryouts and ran to the bathroom in the basement. All nineteen of us crammed into the bright pink room. Clothing flew everywhere as we scrambled to get ready.

The standard uniform for the day was shorts and t-shirts. I wore Mom's YMCA camp shirt and a pair of navy blue knit shorts that were easy to move in. White knee-high athletic socks with a navy-blue stripe near the top of each sock and cloth sneakers completed the ensemble.

Girls trickled out of the bathroom into the gym room. Three high school cheerleaders, including our coach Jeannette, sat behind a metal fold-up table. Each one of them had a pen and a spiral-bound notebook at hand.

Stickers, numbered one to nineteen, were handed out to each hopeful as they approached the table. A smile came to my face. *Seven? That's a lucky number, right?*

Once everyone was ready, the cheerleaders had us form three lines. We ran through the group cheer several times. After we did it once, the front row moved to the back row, and we performed it again. Then we did it one last time with the middle row in front.

Next, we were sorted into random small groups and instructed to do the sideline cheers we'd been taught. At the end of each group's performance, the judges sent some girls to the right side of the room and some to the left.

I studied the two groups. You didn't have to be a rocket scientist to figure which ones were being considered for the squad and who the rejects were. Theresa, Tammy, Sharon, Jane, Gina, and Sheila were in the group to the left. *Not going to end well for them.*

Unless, of course, they actually didn't want to be

cheerleaders. Maybe they felt pressured to try out because everyone else was. Who knows, they could be breathing a sigh of relief this very moment.

The judges put me in the last small group with Connie and Rhonda. We ran through the cheers as instructed, and then Connie was sent to join the group with Patty, Laura, Gail, Bobbi Jo, Brenda, Stacey and Rebecca. That left me and Rhonda.

My heart raced with excitement. *They must be deciding between me and Rhonda.* There were only nine spots on the team, and eight girls stood in the group to the right.

Rhonda and I were asked to run through the group dance one more time. Finishing that, they instructed us to do two more sideline cheers. I cheered like my life was on the line. There was no way I was going down without a fight.

When we finished, the cheerleaders looked at each other, nodded in unison and pointed me towards the group on the right. I bounded over to Bobbi Jo and Patty and gave each of them a hug. Rhonda's shoulders drooped as she made her way to the other group.

The spokesmen for the cheerleaders pointed to our group and said, "Congratulations. You girls are the eighth-grade St. Joseph cheerleading squad for the 1975 to 1976 school year."

Squeals of delight erupted from us. We bounced up and down, and more hugs went around the group. The other girls shuffled out of the room to gather their belongings.

"Cheerleaders," said Jeannette, clapping her hands

to get our attention. "I'd like to get a few practices in before summer vacation. Raise your hand if you're good with that."

All hands shot in the air.

"Cool. We'll start next Saturday. Meet me on the grassy spot at the end of the church parking lot. 10:00 sharp." Our heads nodded eagerly. "You're dismissed. See you next week."

We bounded into the hall, whooping and hollering as we gathered up our gear. I could have leaped for joy. Everything that Richard had said three weeks ago disappeared from my mind.

As we headed towards the stairs to leave the building, someone tapped my shoulder.

"Hey, Allison. I just wanted to say congratulations."

"Thanks, Laura," I replied, trying to hide the surprise in my voice. She'd never gone out of her way to say anything nice to me before. "Same to you."

She didn't make a move to leave. I cocked my head, waiting to hear what else she had to say.

"Anyhow, there's just one thing I wanted to mention to you," she said, crossing her arms in front of her chest. "Stacey, Gail, Rebecca and I were just talking."

Like that was anything different. They were always talking. Or make that gossiping. I leaned toward her expectantly.

"When we start practice next week, you don't have to worry about learning the group cheers."

"What?" My eyes narrowed. "What do you mean by that?"

"Since you were picked last for the squad, it's obvious you're an alternate," she said authoritatively. "It wouldn't be right for you to do the main cheers with the rest of us."

Her eyebrows arched over her oversized plastic glass frames, and she tilted her head slightly to the side. "It's fine if you learn the sideline cheers and stuff, but since you're obviously not as good as the rest of us, we don't want you messing up the dance routines."

My mouth gaped open. Heat crept up my face from my chin to my ears.

"No one said I was an alternate!"

"You were picked last."

"I was picked last because I was in the last group. That doesn't mean everyone else is better than me."

Hands jammed on my hips, voice rising, I continued. "Besides, you're not in charge. Jeannette's the coach. She's the one that makes the decisions."

"She may be our coach, but the other girls nominated me to be captain of the squad," said Laura in a snotty tone. "It's my call."

"Like heck it is. We'll see what Jeannette has to say about this."

Flipping her hair, Laura turned toward the opposite stairway. Fuming, I stood rooted to the floor.

She turned and glanced at me again. "Here's something else to consider. Me and Richard were talking the other day." My stomach dropped to my feet. “He told me he won’t play for St. Joseph’s next year if you’re a cheerleader.”

The sound of rushing waves crashed through my ears. Now Richard had Laura and all the other popular girls ganging up on me.

“Maybe you should just give up your spot on the team and let Rhonda take it. It’d be best for everybody.”

That was the straw that broke the camel’s back. I crossed my arms in front of me and stamped my foot. “No freakin’ way,” I shouted. “I’m not quitting, and you’re not going to be the boss of me. I made the team fair and square, like everyone else. When we get to practice next week, I’m talking to Jeannette.”

Laura flinched. “Fine. Do whatever you want. But when Richard quits, I’m going to tell everybody how selfish you are.”

“Go ahead,” I shot back. “And I’ll tell everybody what a jerk you are.”

Laura rolled her eyes and stomped off.

Leaning against the block wall by the water fountain, my breath came out in gasps. I’d never been so mad in my entire life. *Why is everything going wrong in this crap-show? Nothing ever turns out like I want it to.*

Chapter 52

Arriving early at our first cheerleading practice, I immediately sought out Jeannette. She assured me that she'd address the situation. Sure enough, before we started, she made an announcement that the cheerleading squad had no captain, we were all the same rank, and she called the shots, no one else. I saw Laura's eyes roll.

Even though cheerleading got off to a rocky start, I was glad that I'd made the team. It was more fun than I'd thought it'd be. Hopefully, Mom could catch up on the cheers when she got back into her life.

The third-to-last Friday of the school year, Sister Martha gave us a special assignment in religion class, something she'd heard of at a teacher's convention. We were each given a piece of paper folded vertically with every student's name typed alphabetically, top to bottom, on each half of the sheet.

Sister asked us to fill in the left-hand column with something negative about each person in our class and the right-hand column with something positive about each person.

Seems pointless. Who'd want to hear something bad about themselves? Reading my thoughts, Sister assured us that the negative comments should be taken as constructive criticism that we could learn and grow from. The positive comments would help us truly realize that we were all unique and beloved children of God.

Class time was devoted to the assignment. When it came time to fill in the spot by Richard's name in the left-hand column, I wondered how many synonyms there were for the word jerk. The right-hand column was even more difficult.

It was a moral dilemma. *Do I take the high road and search for something that was remotely good about him, or take the easy route and write "good athlete" like most of the other kids probably were doing?*

Choosing to put that off until the end, I worked my way through the list. The easy task was saying positive things about Mom's friends. They were all nice. I put some thought into each comment to make them slightly different but still personal to them.

The girls in the popular group? Other than Laura, one-on-one, I could get along with any of them.

Overall, the boys in our class, other than Richard, were a good bunch of guys. Some of them were weird; there were no two ways about it. But, that's to be expected for junior high boys. By the time they got to high school, they should come around. For their sake, I hoped so.

With less than two minutes left, I had to write something positive about Richard. Taking a deep breath, I gave into my higher self and wrote, "You're unique and talented. God loves you enough that He died for you."

Handing my paper to Sister, I let my breath out. All the finished sheets in hand, Sister told us she'd compile the answers over the weekend. Monday, she'd give each of us a sheet with the comments written about us. It would be anonymous, so people wouldn't know who wrote what.

Everyone looked forward to getting the sheets back. At the end of the day Monday, Sister Martha handed each of us an envelope with our name on it. "These are to be opened when you get home. You should read them in private."

That suggestion went in one ear and out the other for Vicky and Tammy. Their envelopes were ripped open the moment we stepped off school property.

"Is my hair really that bad?" asked Tammy, running her fingers over her head.

"Why do you say that?" asked Vicky.

"Because at least four people said I have greasy hair."

"Your hair is fine," I reassured her. "People probably just didn't know what to write because they don't know you that well."

There was some truth to the hair comment, but I didn't want her to feel bad. Maybe this would give her the impetus to wash it more than once a week.

"You can tell the things written by the people who aren't my friends," noted Vicky. "It's all the same thing for the good things. She's nice, she's okay. Wait a minute, 'Her dad has a cool car.' Neat! Wonder who wrote that?"

Probably someone who hasn't seen that stupid thing sitting on blocks in their driveway for the last nine months.

"What does your list say, Allison?" asked Tammy.

"I'm going to wait until I get home to read it," I

replied. "I don't feel like looking at it now."

That's a lie if I ever heard one. In reality, I was dying to see the positive comments. I was worried about the negative comments, though.

Reaching my house, I said goodbye to the girls, raced up the driveway, took the concrete porch steps by twos, and flung open the back door. My tennies flew off as I headed straight upstairs without even checking out the snack that Grandma had made.

With the room door shut tightly behind me, I plopped down on the bed, tore the envelope open and read through the negative comments, choosing to save the positive comments for last.

"She's quiet. She's a nerd. Sometimes she talks before she thinks. She can be bossy. She has stringy hair."

Yikes, some of those things were constructive criticism, like Sister Martha had said, but some were kind of mean. Reading down the list, I saw one that stood out. "She's a dog."

"Wow, I wonder who wrote that?" I said out loud. Of course, what else would Richard write? He wasn't the sharpest tool in the shed.

Having made it through all the negative comments, I turned with anticipation to the right column. "She's smart. She's nice. She's one of my best friends." Awww. A smile lit my face. "She's always nice to everybody. She's really good in school. She's a good cheerleader." *So sweet!*

The next comment was like a punch to the gut. "She's a dog, and she'll always be a dog."

I couldn't believe my eyes. Richard was the most

colossal a-hole on the planet. There was no doubt about it. The fact that Sister Martha saw that comment and actually typed it on the sheet flabbergasted me. How could she do that to me? Hadn't she seen all the mean things that Richard had been doing to me all year? What possible good would it do to put his nasty comment on the paper?

Tears rolling down my cheeks, I tore the whole page into tiny shreds. I didn't need a reminder of what a crummy person I was. Flinging myself back onto the bed, I stared at the ceiling for half an hour, tears sliding down the side of my face into my hair.

Finally getting up, I scooped up the paper shreds and went downstairs. Grabbing Mom's lighter off the dining room table, I headed to the garage, crouched on the concrete floor and flicked the lighter on. When the flame appeared, I grabbed the first bit of paper and set it on fire. One by one, I burned every piece. Once they'd disintegrated into a pile of ashes, I fell to the floor, completely spent.

Chapter 53

The next day at school, all the kids talked about their lists. Unlike me, everyone else seemed to love the assignment. They made light of the negative things but were touched by the nice things people wrote about them. Some of the guys had even cut the slips of paper in half and folded the right-hand side into a small rectangle and put them in their wallets.

Listening to the conversations around me, I was glad that people were encouraged by what they read, but I just wanted to forget the whole thing.

As it was the last week of Gym for the school year, Mr. Kovac promised us that we'd get to do something fun in gym. My expectations were low because the last time he said that, we had an entire unit on square dancing. It had been so awkward do-si-doing arm-in-arm with the boys.

Dancing with Richard was the worst. As much as I tried to avoid him, Mr. Kovac warned us that if anybody failed to follow his calls and dance with the person next to us, our phy-ed grades would suffer.

The end of that unit couldn't come fast enough. I swore I'd never listen to another Country Western song for as long as I lived.

Curious as to what fun Mr. Kovac had in store for us today, we headed downstairs to the gym room, chatting as we went. "Maybe we'll get to play scooter ball again," Edward Schultz guessed.

Good lord, I hope not. Scooter ball involved chasing a little ball around the gym floor while seated on a square piece of wood with four roller wheels. Basically, soccer on scooters but with a much smaller ball. It was fun enough, but after watching at least three kids get their fingers run over, my enthusiasm for the sport waned. How many fingers had to get lost before they finally banned that game?

Entering the gym area, we saw mats laid out on the floor. Mr. Kovac lined up the boys and the girls into two queues, shortest to tallest, and then paired everyone up with the person next to them.

"Today, we're going to do Indian leg wrestling," he announced, a grin crossing his face.

The boys gave him a good reception. Wrestling was a popular pastime for them on the playground. Not so much for the girls, so Mr. Kovac had Greg Kohler and David Scherer demonstrate how it worked.

They lay next to each other with their heads on opposite ends of the mat and lined their hips next to each other. When Mr. Kovac said, "Go," the two lifted the leg closest to their opponent straight up three times as he counted down. On the third lift, they wrapped their legs together and tried to flip the other person over. Whoever flipped over his opponent won.

Competitive by nature, I was ready to jump in. Mr. Kovac had everyone do a couple of practice rounds so we could get the hang of it. Each team decided if they were going to wrestle with their left legs or rights legs. He had one pair at a time wrestle while everyone else watched.

Richard and Ronald started the bout. Even though Ronald outweighed him, Richard wore a cocky smirk as he took his position. When Mr. Kovac got down to one, the bout began. They were actually well-matched. It took about twenty seconds before Richard finally got Ronald over.

Gina and Sharon, who were close in size, led off the girls. It didn't take Gina more than five seconds to eliminate Sharon. From there, we went down the line, switching from the boy pairs to the girl pairs.

Despite being vertically challenged, my legs were strong. While I didn't win as quickly as Gina had, I did flip Stacey over. After the first round, those who were eliminated took a seat away from the mats, and the winners paired up with the person next to them.

It was apparent that Gina and Richard were the strongest girl and the strongest boy in our class. I held my own, making it to the fourth round, where I had to face off with Gina. Didn't take much for her to flip me.

As we predicted, Richard and Gina were the overall champions. Everyone clapped at what we assumed was the end of the competition.

Mr. Kovac raised his voice to get everyone's attention. "We need to crown the ultimate leg wrestling champ," he announced. "We're going to have our top boy wrestle our top girl."

Gina's eyes widened like saucers as she stared at her brother. "What?"

"Hey, Mr. Kovac," said Richard. "I don't wanna hurt your sister."

"Trust me, you won't hurt her," he said. "She's a

lot tougher than she looks. I should know."

Gina's face turned crimson.

"Ladies get to choose. Right leg or left leg, Gina?" asked Mr. Kovac.

She glared at her brother and said nothing. That didn't deter him.

"Well, seeing that you're a lefty, we'll have you wrestle left-legged." He pointed to her and Richard, indicating the spot on the mat where they were to match up. Neither of them seemed excited about the prospect.

Even though we knew that it was a mismatch, us girls began a chant. "Gina, Gina, Gina!"

"Rich, Rich, Rich," yelled the boys right back.

"Okay, you two, get in place," said Mr. Kovac, positioning himself as ref.

Richard dropped to the mat. Gina hesitated, like she wished she was anywhere else in the world at the moment.

There was no holding this train back. "On the mat," said Mr. Kovac.

Heaving a sigh, Gina lined up next to Richard. Everyone started yelling and cheering, and Mr. Kovac began the count. "Three...two...one...!"

The two wrapped their left legs around each other's, and to everyone's surprise, they went back and forth for at least twenty-five seconds, the momentum changing every few seconds. They were giving it their all. Sweat beaded up on Richard's forehead. Gina's lips were sealed tight as she pushed her leg down with all her might.

Out of the blue, Gina slammed her leg completely down to the mat, and Richard flipped over, landing face down.

Every girl jumped up, whooping and cheering. When Gina stood up, we gathered around her, hugging her and slapping her back.

The boys stared in disbelief. Richard lay on his stomach for a few seconds, got up to his knees and onto his feet. He pushed through the crowd of boys and went to get his shoes.

Dejectedly, the other boys followed suit as the celebration continued. Some of the girls said this was even better than when Billie Jean King beat Bobby Riggs in tennis in the Battle of the Sexes. Whatever that was. All I knew was that Gina's victory over Richard was the talk of the school the next day.

Chapter 54

I couldn't wipe the smile off my face for the next twenty-four hours. The topic of the wrestling match came up several times during the school day. Sister Cecilia and Sister Martha heard numerous versions of the story from us girls as we reveled in girl power. For once, all of us were on the same team.

The good mood stayed with me through Thursday too. Feeling light and happy, I enjoyed every moment of the day. That afternoon, I had an ah-ha moment. I realized what was happening. Actually, what wasn't happening to be more specific.

Richard had stopped picking on me. As a matter of fact, he wasn't interacting with me at all. I had the impression that he was actually going out of his way to avoid me. I couldn't believe my luck.

The only explanation that I could think of was him losing the wrestling match. Gina had completely humiliated him. Was he avoiding me because he knew that me and Gina were good friends?

That theory made sense. By the end of the day, I was convinced that it was true. The torment that I'd gone through for the whole school year was over. I wanted to sing aloud with joy.

As a test, when the final bell rang one day, I purposely followed Richard down the back steps, quickening my pace to reach the landing at the same time he did. Garnering his attention, he turned, and when his eyes met mine, he turned his head and continued down the steps. I flew past him, rounded the corner, took the next set of steps two at a time, and then jumped the final set of stairs to reach the glass doors.

Pushing them open, I ran outside. *Free at last!* I didn't know if I should laugh or cry. If I'd had an umbrella, I'd have done the *Singing in the Rain* dance.

Twirling around, I glimpsed Richard inside the glass doors and came to a dead stop. He had a sixth-grader cornered, his meaty hands wrapped around the lapel of the kid's checkered button-up shirt.

What the heck? I had no idea what they were talking about, but from my vantage point, the smaller boy looked like he wanted no part of the conversation.

Something inside me snapped. I rushed back into the building, yanked open the glass door and confronted Richard.

"Get your hands off him, Richard!"

Recognizing my voice, he replied. "Go home, Allison. This is none of your business."

Finding strength that I didn't know I possessed, I grabbed Richard's arm and pulled him away from the kid.

"Stop picking on him," I yelled.

All I got in reply from Richard was a snotty look. I turned back to the younger boy. "Don't let him do this to you. Richard thinks he's all that and then some, but he's just a big bully. And he only picks on kids who are smaller than him. When he's in a real fight, he loses. Heck, he even got beat in leg wrestling by a girl in our class."

The kid's eyes widened. He crept closer to the front door of the building. "You can get going," I said. "But, before you leave, if I tell you something, will you remember?"

He nodded solemnly.

"You are braver than you believe, stronger than you seem, and smarter than you think."

A smile lit his face. I pushed the glass door open, and he scampered out.

I squared up in front of Richard. His arms were crossed, and the typical arrogant look was on his face.

"One more thing, Richard. I have no idea what your problem is and why you feel compelled to torment kids who are smaller than you. But, if I ever witness you pulling any of these stunts on anybody again, I'm sending my brothers after you. How'd you like to have a taste of your own medicine?"

Richard snorted and brushed past me as he stomped out the door.

Who knew if what I said would make a difference in his life, but I was pretty sure he'd leave that guy alone from now on. So, if nothing else, it was worth standing up to Richard for that.

The last week of school, I kept my eye on Richard. I wasn't kidding about siccing Uncle Howard on him. If Howard had known what Richard had put me through the whole school year, he'd probably beat the crap out of him just for that alone. As much as Mom and her siblings squabbled, they stuck up for each other out in the real world.

To my surprise, though, the message appeared to have gotten through to Richard. While we had no interactions with each other, he seemed to be getting along fairly with the rest of the kids in the class, even the kids in the not-popular groups.

On the last day of school, each grade got to do something special. The eighth-graders were going to see *The Island of the Blue Dolphins* at the movie theater. A couple of classes had picnics in the park. The seventh graders voted to go to Round Lake.

With Father Dom as our chaperone, we rode a school bus to the county park, leaving all the windows closed so we'd get nice and toasty by the time we got there. The lake would be freezing. We wanted to be as hot as possible before we jumped in.

Everyone wore their swimsuits under their clothes. Piling from the bus, we whipped off our shorts and shirts and ran towards the water. The faster we got completely wet, the less chance we'd back out.

Playing swim tag, throwing footballs and Frisbees around, and hanging out talking in the water was a blast. Someone suggested that we play chicken. Father Dom volunteered to be a base with one kid on his shoulders, while Lawrence's dad, who was also a chaperone, had another kid on his shoulders. The idea was to push or pull your opponent off the shoulders of the adult without getting knocked off yourself. Brenda got dunked when I pulled her off Mr. Coopman's shoulders.

Wading deeper into the lake, kids climbed on Father Dom's shoulders and dove into the water. My form wasn't great, but it was fun.

After our picnic lunch, we had to clean up right away to catch the bus back to school. Near the picnic tables was a big wooden sign that had "NO DOGS ALLOWED" carved into it.

A couple girls had the idea of posing the class in front of the sign for a picture. Beach towels were draped over the sign, so only the word DOGS was visible.

We arranged ourselves in a lopsided pyramid in front of the sign, and everyone did their best imitation of a dog. Father Dom set up the shot with a promise to make sure it would be in the next church bulletin.

Being one of the lightest kids in the class, I got the highest spot on the pyramid. Pulling my hands up to my chest and folding my fingers over, so they looked like paws, I glanced down to see everyone else's poses.

Even Richard joined in. It was neat seeing everyone in our class mixed in with everyone else. No popular group, no not-popular group. Just the friends and classmates they'd been since they'd started school together.

For better or for worse, I was glad that I got to know everybody in Mom's class and see what it was like growing up in her day. I'd always remember each one of them and how they were as seventh-graders.

"Cheese!"

In unison, we all smiled for Father Dom. The bulb on the camera flashed, and not two seconds later, the pyramid collapsed, sending all of us tumbling to the ground.

On the way down, my head slammed into Jane's shoulder. A familiar sensation washed over me. It was as though I had fallen asleep instantaneously, with me looking on as everything went on around me, but no longer physically there.

Stars drifted through my head. I lay still for a few seconds, shook my head slightly to chase the orbs away, and cautiously opened my eyes.

Above me, I saw the white bedroom ceiling. I drew in a breath and let out a long sigh. Tilting my head to my right, a taupe wall came into view. My mouth gaped open.

"Good morning, Morgan." The bed squeaked with the weight of a body being lowered onto it. "How are you feeling today?"

My eyes shot completely open. I pivoted my head toward the sound.

"Mom?" I squeezed my eyes shut and opened them again. "It really is you!"

Tears welled up in my eyes as Mom engulfed me in her arms. I wrapped my arms around her back.

"You had me worried last night," she said, running her hand through my hair. "Sounded like you were having some intense dreams."

"You can say that again."

She ran her fingers through my hair, and when her hand touched the side of my head, I winced. My eyes opened wider. The goose egg. It was there! I'd never felt so happy in my life.

"Mom, you're the most remarkable person I've ever met!" I said, hugging her even tighter.

"You must've hit your head a lot harder than I thought," she said with a laugh. "We should probably take you to immediate care and get that looked at."

"I'm fine, Mom, really I am."

Her eyes bright, she smiled at me. Had I been gone a year? Maybe so. Mom looked so different to me. More sophisticated or confident or something. Leaning back, I admired the outfit she wore.

"Mom, I've had a lot of time to think. And, I want you to know how grateful I am for everything you do for me. For the boys and Dad too."

"That's sweet of you to say, Morgan."

I couldn't stop staring at her. She was beautiful. Inside and out. How hadn't I noticed that before?"

"If you're sure you're feeling all right, you should get up now. It's not every day that a girl starts her first day of middle school."

Middle school? I hadn't missed a whole year of my life? *Thank you for the re-do, God! I promise this time around to do my best to be grateful for every moment you give me, good or bad.*

"Mom, I had the craziest experience," I looked deep into her eyes to gauge her reaction. "Maybe it was a dream, but it sure felt real. I had the chance to live your life for a year when you were in seventh grade."

"Really? We should compare notes," she replied with a laugh.

"That would be great! Do you think we can go to the coffee shop tonight after dinner and hang out for a while?"

"You sure you want to do that with me and not your friends?" she asked with a teasing note in her voice.

"Absolutely!" I paused for a moment. "You really are strong, Mom. I never knew how strong until I went through this."

"We're both strong, honey," she said sincerely. "We come from solid stock. You made it through a lot of things yourself, and you survived."

Her smile was cryptic. My brow wrinkled as I tried to decipher her meaning.

"What doesn't kill us, makes us stronger, doesn't it, Morgan?"

I returned her smile. "It really does, Mom. It really does."

THE END

Acknowledgments

For my mom, Jacqueline Purcell, my dad, Kieran Purcell, and my brothers Gordon Purcell and Rodney Purcell, it was an honor and a blessing to grow up in the family that I did. We had our share of ups and downs, but the good outweighed the bad. What didn't kill us made us stronger! I couldn't have asked for better parents, better brothers or a better life growing up. Love you all!

For my husband John Lauer, our children Stephanie, Nicholas, Samantha and Elizabeth, their significant others, our grandchildren, and my entire extended family for their continued love, support and encouragement.

For my publisher Ellen Gable Hrkach of Full Quiver Publishing for taking a chance on me once again as I venture into another genre of writing.

For James Hrkach of Full Quiver Publishing for creating this eye-catching and enticing book cover.

For Brad Birkholz for shooting the flower photo that was used as the background for the front cover.

For Michelle Buckman, who gave me the idea to change the story from a coming-of-age memoir to a time-travel novel so that readers from middle school age through adult would be able to relate to and enjoy this tale.

For friends and family from the 1970s whose pictures were used to create these amazing front and back book covers:

Deb Sell is pictured with me on the front cover, circa fall 1975.

On the back cover, the picture on the left is my seventh-grade school picture.

The middle picture is my group of forever friends having a fun day gathered by the front porch of the house in which I spent a good portion of my growing-up years. From left to right on the front porch is me, Janelle Darling, Betsy Ross, Deb Sell and her sister Cindy Daul. Julie Seis is pictured standing in front of the porch.

The picture on the right was taken on the day my brother Rodney graduated from St. John School in the spring of 1974. Rodney is on the left, I'm in the middle, and our oldest brother Gordon is on the right.

A special thanks to Julie Seis, with whom I've been friends since we met in Sr. Leonita's class in first grade. Julie was our maid of honor when John and I were married in 1981, and she is our son Nicholas' godmother. Julie has shown me what it truly means to be a best friend.

To Full Quiver Publishing for its dedication to bringing books to the public that entertain, enlighten and bring readers closer to Christ.

About the Author

Amanda Lauer is the author of the best-selling *Heaven Intended* Civil War series. *A World Such as Heaven Intended* won the 2016 YA CALA award. Lauer won Best Writer 2020 (Red Letter Awards) for her work on the movie *The Islands.* She collaborated on the recently released children's book *Dubbie: The Double Headed Eagle.* Her story *Lucky and Blessed,* part of the anthology *Treasures: Visible & Invisible,* was released March 1, 2021. Over the last twenty years, Lauer has had more than 1,500 articles published in newspapers and magazines throughout the United States. She and her husband John have been married forty years and have four grown children, two sons-in-law, a daughter-in-law, and seven remarkable grandchildren.

Published by
Full Quiver Publishing
PO Box 244
Pakenham ON K0A2X0
Canada

Made in USA - Kendallville, IN
1238061_9781987970227
02.23.2021 0837